BORN

Mueller cleared his throat and went on talking as if I hadn't said a thing. "On the other hand, Donald dropped out of school the day he turned sixteen. Believe me, I wasn't a bit sorry to lose *him*." He paused and gave me another long hard look. "I wonder which of your brothers you take after, Gordon."

It was just the way I'd known it would be—everybody remembered my father and my brothers. They all expected me to turn out every bit as bad as they had. The only question was, whose path would I follow? Would I become the town drunk? Would I drop out of school and blow up gas stations? Would I desert if another war started?

When I didn't say anything, Mueller frowned. "I plan to keep an eye on you, Gordon. Any sign of misbehavior and I'll come down on you hard. Is that clear?"

"Yes, sir," I muttered. His message was clear. It was my first day at Hyattsdale High, and the principal already hated me.

Other Novels by Mary Downing Hahn

The Ghost of Crutchfield Hall

Closed for the Season

All the Lovely Bad Ones

Deep and Dark and Dangerous

Witch Catcher

Janey and the Famous Author

The Old Willis Place

Hear the Wind Blow

Anna on the Farm

Promises to the Dead

Anna All Year Round

The Gentleman Outlaw and Me—Eli

Look for Me by Moonlight

Time for Andrew

The Wind Blows Backward

Stepping on the Cracks

Following My Own Footsteps

The Dead Man in Indian Creek

The Doll in the Garden

Tallahassee Higgins

Wait Till Helen Comes

Daphne's Book

AS EVER, GORDY

by Mary Downing Hahn

Houghton Mifflin Harcourt

Boston New York

 Published in the United States by Sandpiper, an imprint of Houghton Mifflin Harcourt Publishing Company. Originally published in hardcover in the United States by Clarion Books, an imprint of Houghton Mifflin Harcourt Publishing Company, 1998.

www.hmhco.com

The Library of Congress has cataloged the hardcover edition as follows:
Hahn, Mary Downing.
As ever, Gordy / Mary Downing Hahn.
p. cm.
A sequel to: Following my own footsteps.
Summary: When he and his younger sister move in with their older brother after their grandmother dies, thirteen-year-old Gordy finds himself caught between the boy he was when he lived with his abusive father and the boy his grandmother was helping him become.
[1. Behavior—Fiction. 2. Brothers and sisters—Fiction.] I. Title.
PZ7.H1256As 1998
[Fic]—dc21 7-18913

ISBN: 978-0-395-83627-9 hardcover
ISBN: 978-0-547-54955-2 paperback

Manufactured in the United States of America
DOH 10 9 8 7 6 5 4

4500572643

For all the College Park kids,
especially Ann, Connie, and Jack

1

Just about the time I thought my life was going pretty well, something happened that changed everything. I should have seen it coming, sensed it in the air the way you smell smoke before you see fire, but I had no inkling. None at all.

As a matter of fact, when the news came, I was in English class, staring out the window as if I had forever to sit there studying clouds. Mr. Isaacson stood at the blackboard, showing us how to diagram sentences. Like most grammar lessons, it bored me to death, but not my friend William. He wrote down everything Mr. Isaacson said. That's how William was—too smart for his own good. Later I'd copy his notes, but I had better things to think about now—the way Nancy Jean Allen's hair curled on the back of her neck, the Friday basketball game, the war movie I hoped to see at the Palace on Saturday, maybe with Nancy Jean.

Just as Mr. Isaacson fit a participle into the diagram,

someone knocked on the door. Like everybody else, I stopped what I was doing and watched Mr. Isaacson go into a huddle with the school secretary. Suddenly they both stared right at me. A couple of kids noticed. William turned around in his seat, a worried look on his face, but Billy Brown grinned and ran a finger across his throat. The whole class, including me, thought I was in trouble. But for the life of me, I couldn't think of a single bad thing I'd done recently.

"Gordy," Mr. Isaacson said, "you'd better get your books and go to the office with Miss Spurles."

It wasn't what he said that scared me but the way he said it. His voice was soft and low, not a speck of anger in it, and his face was sorrowful. The whole class watched me stand up. Nobody was grinning now. Like me, they knew this was serious business.

I walked down the hall beside Miss Spurles, wanting to ask her what was wrong but too scared to open my mouth. Suppose June had been hit by a car on her way to school? Suppose my big brother Donny had wrecked that old jalopy he was so proud of? Worst of all, suppose my father was waiting in the principal's office, come all the way from California to tell me Mama was sick and needed me?

At the door to Mr. Nelson's office, Miss Spurles paused and laid her hand on my shoulder. "I'm afraid it's bad news, Gordy," she said in a low voice. "And I want you to know I'm real sorry about it."

I nodded and swallowed hard. Mr. Nelson was standing behind his desk, looking at me with sad eyes like everyone else. Slowly I walked a little closer and stopped in front of him, dreading to hear what he had to say. At least the old man wasn't anywhere in sight.

Mr. Nelson cleared his throat, like he'd lost his voice and was trying to find it. "Gordy," he said, "I got a call from your neighbor a few minutes ago." He paused to clear his throat again. "Mrs. Sullivan told me your grandmother was taken to the hospital this morning. A heart attack, she said."

For all the sense I could make of what Mr. Nelson was saying, he might as well have been speaking German or Italian. Strange as it sounds, I'd never once thought the bad news had anything to do with Grandma.

"There must be some mistake," I said, swallowing the cold lump in my throat. "Grandma was fine when I left for school, she couldn't have had a heart attack, she's as strong as horse, she, she—why, she—"

My voice ran on and on all by itself. I swear my brain had shut down like I'd thrown a switch or blown a fuse.

When I finally stopped babbling, Mr. Nelson said, "Your brother Donny is on his way to get you. He should be here any minute now." He cleared his throat again. "I'm truly sorry, Gordy. Mrs. Aitcheson was a fine woman. We taught together for many years before she retired. I admired her more than I can say."

Though it worried me, I didn't dare ask Mr. Nelson why he'd said Grandma *was* a fine woman. I'd convinced myself Grandma was in the hospital but not too bad off. Soon she'd be home. In the meantime, I'd look after June and keep the house tidy. Maybe I'd buy Grandma some flowers or candy. Chocolates were her biggest weakness—once she started eating them, she just couldn't stop. I figured I had enough allowance left to get her a big fancy box of her favorites.

I was thinking about the chocolates when Donny showed up. Slinging one arm around my shoulders, he gave me a fast hug, something he never did, and hustled me out of school.

"Hurry up," he said. "I told Mrs. Sullivan I'd bring you to her house. June's already there."

I slid into the front seat beside my brother, smelling the familiar smells of old leather and cigarette smoke. "When are we going to the hospital to see Grandma?"

Donny stopped fooling with the ignition and stared at me. "Didn't they tell you?"

The cold lump I'd choked down in Nelson's office came back, filling my throat like an ice cube I'd swallowed without meaning to. "Grandma had a heart attack, she's in the hospital, but she'll be home soon," I said, stringing the words together as fast as I could. "I hope she doesn't feel too bad to eat chocolate. Maybe we could stop on the way to the hospital and pick up some at the drugstore. She likes those big fancy boxes, the ones with lots of different kinds. Her favorites have nuts in the middle, she always eats those first, then she—"

"Gordy, for God's sake!" Donny yelled. "Shut up and listen to me. Grandma's dead. She died on the way to the hospital!"

The words I was about to say froze on my tongue, and I sat there, too stunned to breathe. Donny might as well have hit me over the head with a two-by-four. Grandma couldn't be dead. It wasn't possible. I'd have known she was gone, I'd have felt her passing. Donny was mistaken. He had to be—or else he was lying.

I turned to him. "It's not true, Donny, it's not true!" My voice began as a whisper but ended as a shout. "You're a liar!"

Hurling myself at him, I started hitting him, punching him as hard as I could, cussing up a blue streak. I was so mad I wanted to kill him.

Donny shoved me against the car door and held me there. "Quit it, Gordy," he said. "Hitting me isn't going to change anything."

The look on my brother's face took the fight right out of me. I stopped struggling and slumped against the door. "Maybe it's a mistake, maybe they mixed her up with someone else," I whispered. "I saw this movie once—"

Donny pulled me close and hugged me, squashing my nose against his old army jacket. "There's no mistake, Gordy. Mrs. Sullivan called me at work and told me. I checked with the hospital just to make sure."

As much as I wanted to keep on arguing, I knew Donny was telling me the truth. The worst possible thing had happened, and I'd been too dumb to see it coming. Hadn't prepared for it, either. Living with Grandma had spoiled me. I'd forgotten to watch for the bad stuff that waited around every corner.

For the first time in my whole life, I broke down and cried—me, Gordy Smith, bawling like a baby. Nothing my father ever did to me had made me feel this bad. Black eyes, cuts, bruises—sooner or later they stopped hurting, but not this. The one person I trusted, the one person I counted on, was gone, and she'd left a hole in my heart big enough to drive a truck through.

Donny muttered a few words meant to make me feel better and then went back to cranking the engine. I hadn't seen him look so glum since he'd come home from the war.

By the time the old Ford started, I'd almost stopped crying, but my voice still didn't sound right. "Where are we going?" I asked.

"To Mrs. Sullivan's house. She wants you and June to stay with her and William till everything's settled."

"Why can't you look after us?" I stared at Donny, mad all over again. Surprised, too. "We don't need Mrs. Sullivan. We're a family, you and June and me. We—"

"No dice, Gordy." Donny cut me off. "Dave and I are leaving for Tulsa soon. You know that, we've talked about it before."

"But everything's different now." I tried to keep my voice steady. If Donny got the idea I was a snotty-nosed bawl baby, he wouldn't want anything to do with me. "You can't just go off and leave us. It's not right."

Donny busied himself lighting a cigarette. "What's wrong with staying with Mrs. Sullivan? She's a nice lady."

"Nice?" I snorted. "She hates me, and you know it."

Donny gave me a look that meant cut the bull, but it was true. When I'd first come to live with Grandma, Mrs. Sullivan thought I was the worst kid she'd ever met—rude and ugly and dumb, cussing and fighting, acting mean. Back then, William was still crippled from polio, and she'd done her best to keep him away from me. Now that he was walking, she'd let up a little, but she was far from crazy about me.

"You'll only be there for a week or so," Donny went on. "And then, after that . . ." His voiced trailed off as if he had no idea what to say next.

"After that, what?" I prompted him. "Where do June and I go?"

Donny turned the corner and slowed to a stop in front of William's house. "Don't worry. Something will turn up."

That was easy for Donny to say. He was old enough to take care of himself. But I was only thirteen. And June had just turned nine. We could end up in an orphanage—or someplace even worse.

"What if it's the old man who turns up? What if he wants to haul June and me off to California?" I grabbed Donny's sleeve to keep him from getting out of the car. "Tell me you won't let him. Promise you'll take us to Tulsa if he comes for us."

Donny pulled his arm away, but he didn't open the door. "Fat chance of him showing up. We don't even know where the SOB is."

I closed my eyes and tried to convince myself Donny was right. We hadn't heard diddlysquat from our parents for over a year. Not a letter, not a phone call, not even a postcard. The day they left for California, they wrote June and me out of their lives.

Nobody missed the old man, but June still fretted about Mama. Even cried for her late at night when she thought nobody heard. I told my sister to forget her. Don't think about her, I said. Don't talk about her.

But no matter how hard I tried to follow my own advice, Mama's sad face had a way of turning up in my dreams. So did the old man's ugly mug. He came to me in nightmares, the kind that keep you awake for hours, sweating and scared, heart pounding, telling yourself he's not really downstairs getting drunk on cheap whiskey.

Donny poked me hard in the ribs. "Are you listening? I'm telling you something important, Gordy."

I scowled at my brother, but he was right to be sore. While he'd been jawing away, I'd been too busy thinking my own thoughts to listen.

Donny took a deep drag on his cigarette. "Like I just said, call Stu. Tell him what's happened. He'll do right by you and June."

"That's the worst idea I ever heard. Stu's already got Barbara and her kid to worry about. What makes you think he'd want June and me?"

"Because Stu's Stu," Donny said. "Responsible. All heart. The perfect family man."

He grinned, happy he'd solved the problem. Let Stu deal with June and me. He, Donny, was off the hook, free to hit the road for Tulsa.

I felt like punching him again. But what was the use? He wasn't about to change his plans. Not for June and me, not for anybody.

"You like Stu," Donny went on. "And that wife of his is one good-looking dame. At least she was the last time I saw her."

"Stu's okay. So's Barbara," I mumbled. "It's College Hill I hate. When we left, I swore I'd never go back—not unless I got rich and famous."

Donny laughed. "I hate to tell you, kid, but you're a long way from either."

"So are you."

"Just wait till I strike oil in Oklahoma, Gordo. I'll be rolling in dough."

"I'm not holding my breath."

Donny didn't say anything. Maybe he hadn't heard me. He was already halfway up the Sullivans' sidewalk.

I followed him, keeping my head down. Next door was Grandma's empty house, but I didn't look at it. It hurt too much to think about her not being there, not *ever* being there. No more cookies after school, no more long talks at the dinner table, no more singing while we washed the dishes. All gone. Just like that.

I wanted to ask Donny if life got better when you grew up, but I was afraid to hear the answer.

2

Mrs. Sullivan came to the door, one finger pressed to her mouth to shush us. "June's asleep on the couch," she whispered. "After I brought her home from school, the poor child wore herself out crying."

Donny looked as relieved as I felt. Much as we loved June, neither one of us wanted the job of comforting her. Once she started crying, nothing could stop her . . . except sleep.

"I'm so sorry about your grandmother," Mrs. Sullivan went on in a low voice. "I can't tell you how much I'll miss her. Florence was a wonderful neighbor, always good to William and me."

She paused to blow her nose and then invited Donny to stay awhile. "I've got a pot of coffee on the stove."

Donny edged toward the door. "Thanks," he said, "but I have some business to attend to, Mrs. Sullivan. I'll take a rain check, okay?"

I stood at the hall window and watched Donny drive away. I guessed he didn't want to be around when June woke up. Or maybe he just wasn't comfortable in Mrs. Sullivan's house. I felt a little uneasy there myself. I worried about breaking one of her little china figurines or tracking mud on the carpet or letting slip a cuss word by accident. She was awful particular about things.

When my brother was out of sight, Mrs. Sullivan took me to the kitchen and fixed us each a bowl of thick, gloppy cream of mushroom soup. While we ate, she asked me for Mama's phone number. She wanted to tell her the sad news so she could come home for the funeral.

Instead of answering, I poked my soup with my spoon and watched it shudder in the bowl like it was alive—an old gray slimy thing you might find in the corner of a dark, damp basement. I hated to tell Mrs. Sullivan I had no idea where Mama was, let alone what her phone number might be.

Mrs. Sullivan reached across the table and touched my hand. "I have to call your mother, Gordy," she said as if I hadn't heard her ask the first time.

I kept my eyes on that soup like I thought it might crawl out of the bowl and smother me. "Mama's in California," I said, "but I don't know exactly where. Bakersfield, maybe. My father had a job there, but he—well, he could be working someplace else by now."

It made no sense to tell Mrs. Sullivan how many jobs the old man could have gone through in a couple of years if he'd started drinking again.

"I see." From the sound of her voice, I knew Mrs. Sullivan didn't see. Couldn't see. What sort of boy didn't know where his own mother was? Or, worse yet, what sort of mother didn't give a hoot where her son was?

"My brother Stu lives in Maryland," I told her. "Maybe we should call him."

Mrs. Sullivan wrote down Stu's number. "Do you want to call him yourself, Gordy?"

I started poking at the soup again. "Would you mind telling him about Grandma? And then letting me talk to him?"

She patted my hand again and left the kitchen. A few seconds later I heard her dialing the phone. To keep from hearing what she said to Stu, I carried the dirty dishes to the sink, scraped my soup into the garbage can, and started running the water.

By the time Mrs. Sullivan came to tell me Stu wanted to talk to me, I'd washed the lunch dishes—which both pleased and surprised her. I doubt she'd counted on me to help with chores, but Grandma had taught me a thing or two. No reason a boy couldn't take his turn washing dishes, she'd said; my hands worked just the same as June's.

When I picked up the phone, Stu began by saying how sorry he was, but he soon got to the point. "Barbara and I want you and June to live with us," he said. "We haven't got much room, but we'll be glad to have you."

I held the phone a little tighter and took a deep breath. While I'd been washing the dishes, I'd come up with a great idea. "What if you all moved down here instead?" I asked. "Grandma's house is real big, and just wait till you see the backyard—there's a vegetable garden and a swing set and plenty of room for Brent to play. Barbara'd love it, and so would you. Why, it's practically a mansion, Stu, even nicer than Barbara's parents' house. It's—"

"I know you're happy in Grandville, Gordy," Stu cut in, "but I'm taking classes at the university, I have a job. I can't drop everything and come down there. I—"

This time I interrupted him. "There's a college just a few miles from Grandville, Stu. The University of North Carolina in Chapel Hill. William says it's much better than the University of stupid Maryland. He says—"

"I'm sorry, Gordy," Stu said, "but I can't do it. You'll have to come here."

And that was that. I slammed the phone down and went upstairs to William's room. Mrs. Sullivan put out a hand to stop me but changed her mind. Maybe she figured I needed some time alone. She was right.

I flung myself in a chair and pondered my future. In College Hill I'd have to face a bunch of people who knew everything there was to know about the Smith family—the dump we'd lived in down at the end of Davis Road; my father being hauled off to jail, drunk and ugly and smelling like a skunk; Mama's busted arm and black eyes. Poor white trash, that's what they thought of us. I'd be as welcome as a dog with rabies.

I must have fallen asleep worrying because the next thing I knew, William was shaking my shoulder and telling me it was time for supper.

Mrs. Sullivan had fixed fried chicken and mashed potatoes, but they weren't anywhere near as good as Grandma's. We sat at the table and picked at the food, but nobody ate much. Didn't talk, either. Every now and then June let out a sob, and Mrs. Sullivan tried to comfort her. Although there was cherry pie for dessert, nobody wanted any.

The next day, Donny met us at the funeral parlor for the viewing. He'd seen plenty of dead people in the war, but neither William, June, nor I had ever had the experience. From the look on their faces, I knew the two of them were just as scared as I was.

The first thing I saw was flowers, lots and lots of flowers, smelling as sweet and strong as perfume, so many of them they almost hid the coffin. I remembered driving past a cemetery once with Grandma. They'd just finished burying somebody, and the new grave was covered with flowers—funeral sprays, Grandma called them. "Dead flowers for dead people," she'd said. "How appropriate."

The funeral director beckoned to June and me. "Come say good-bye to your grandmother, children," he said, as if we were too young to understand the difference between dying and going on a long trip.

My sister hung back, her hand in mine as cold as death, but Mrs. Sullivan gently nudged her forward. "Go on, honey," she whispered.

The two of us walked slowly to the coffin. Grandma

lay still, her eyes closed, her long, thin hands clasped on her chest. Someone had curled her hair and made up her face with rouge and lipstick. Grandma would have been as mad as the dickens if she could have seen what they'd done to her.

When June started crying, the funeral director touched her head and whispered, "Your grandmother looks so peaceful, she could be sleeping."

June stared at the man, her eyes wide. "Is she going to wake up?"

"Why, no, dear, I'm afraid not. I only meant—"

I put my arm around June to hush her. It seemed to me the fool ought to have known better than to tell a little kid something like that. Get her hopes up and all. Maybe I'd come back tomorrow and write a few cuss words on his sidewalk.

The funeral director frowned at me. "Kneel down and say a prayer," he whispered. "It's the proper thing to do."

Keeping a firm grip on June's arm, I dropped to my knees beside the coffin, but I swear I couldn't think of a thing to say to God. He who was supposed to hear the sparrow's fall had let Grandma die long before I was ready to let her go. Long before she was ready to go, too.

Instead of praying, I studied Grandma. This close, her face looked more like wax than flesh, and her sweet talcum smell was gone, replaced by a whiff of something not quite so nice. Even though her eyes were closed, I was suddenly scared she was watching me from beyond, measuring me, worrying I was going to forget everything she'd taught me.

Jerking June to her feet, I backed away from the coffin and went to stand beside Donny. I silently promised Grandma I'd try to behave, I'd do my best to stay out of trouble. No smoking, no cussing, no fighting. But there was no hiding the fact I might not be able to keep my word once I was back in College Hill.

After the funeral director thought we'd had enough time alone with Grandma, he began ushering other people into the room.

The crowd was bigger than I'd thought it would be. Grandma had never been what you'd call sociable. She didn't throw dinner parties or play cards or belong to the Women's Club, preferring to work in the garden or sit on the porch and read, but she'd taught school in Grandville for over forty years before she retired. It seemed none of her students had ever forgotten her. They gathered together, talking in hushed voices about how she'd acted out the witch scene in *Macbeth* every year when they studied Shakespeare. She'd never raised her voice, she'd never shamed anybody, she'd been strict but fair, she'd had a dry sense of humor. In short, they'd learned more English from Mrs. Aitcheson than from any other teacher they'd ever had.

It made me feel good to hear them, and I hoped somehow Grandma was listening, too. She'd have been tickled pink.

The funeral was Friday. Since Grandma hadn't been a churchgoer, the service was held at the undertaker's.

I don't know where they found the minister, but he obviously hadn't known Grandma. For one thing, he called her Flora Atkinson instead of Florence Aitcheson. I was about to stand up and correct him, but Mrs. Sullivan grabbed my arm and shook her head. Later I decided she was right to stop me. Saying something would have just made it worse.

Afterward, we followed the hearse across town to Cedar Hill Cemetery. The line of cars was so long it must have tied up traffic for blocks. Or maybe all the cars in town were in the procession and there wasn't any traffic to tie up.

At the cemetery, we gathered around the grave, and the minister read a part from the Bible that tells about man's being born of woman—how short his life is and how full of trouble. At least he got that part right.

When the minister finished saying his piece, we each dropped a handful of dirt on Grandma's coffin. The thud made my insides ache. I hoped Grandma couldn't hear it. Overhead, the sky seemed bigger and higher than usual. Emptier, too, as if all the clouds had shrunk away from the earth. Crows cawed in the woods. The wind made a high, sad sound in the treetops. It was the lonesomest day of my life.

The others walked back to their cars and began to drive away, but I stayed where I was. How could I leave Grandma here?

Mrs. Sullivan touched my shoulder. "It's time to go, Gordy," she said softly.

"Let me stay awhile," I said. "I'll walk home later."

She shook her head. "I know how you feel, but Florence isn't alone, Gordy. See the names on the tombstones? Your grandfather's resting place is right beside hers."

I looked at the headstone. *Joseph H. Aitcheson, Beloved Husband of Florence Mary Aitcheson, 3 February 1875—11 March 1931.* My grandfather—I'd never even laid eyes on him.

Mrs. Sullivan pointed to a nearby cross, carved with the name Myers. "Florence's mother and father are buried there—her grandparents, too," she told me. "The Aitchesons and the Myerses go way back in Grandville. Your grandmother has plenty of company."

I read the names and dates on the stones. Aitchesons here, Myerses there. My relatives, too, all of them, but considering they were dead, I didn't see how they'd be any comfort to anyone, least of all to Grandma.

"We'd better leave now," Mrs. Sullivan said softly. "The wind is blowing hard enough to give a person double pneumonia."

Though I still didn't want to go, I let Mrs. Sullivan lead me to the car. I looked back once and was sorry I did. Two men carrying shovels came out from wherever they'd been waiting and started filling in the grave. Too heartsick to watch, I put my arm around June and let her sob on my shoulder. I wished I could cry, too, but all the tears in the world wouldn't bring Grandma back.

Besides, I had to be brave for June. That's what Grandma would have expected.

3

The day before we left Grandville, Mrs. Sullivan called Donny, June, and me together to tell us about Grandma's will. I joined them at the kitchen table, but I wasn't interested in what Mrs. Sullivan had to say. It was Grandma I wanted, not her money.

"Everything is to be divided equally between you, Stu, June, and Gordy," Mrs. Sullivan told Donny, "but it will take a while to settle matters. The house and furniture must be sold, the taxes paid, and so on."

Taking a deep breath, she added, "Your grandmother was a wealthy woman and she had no debts, so you should each receive a fairly large sum."

Beside me, Donny tensed. As much as he'd loved Grandma, it was clear he was excited about money coming his way.

Turning to June and me, Mrs. Sullivan said, "Some of your share is available now to help Stu take care of you. Your grandmother put the rest into a trust fund."

"What about Mama?" June asked. "Didn't Grandma leave her anything?"

Mrs. Sullivan rearranged the papers the lawyer had given her. "I'm afraid not," she said in a low voice.

"Poor Mama," June whispered, her eyes brimming with tears.

Donny and I glanced at each other. It was no surprise to us. Grandma hadn't mentioned Mama's name once since Mama had gone to California with the old man.

"Mama should've stayed here with us," I muttered, "like Grandma wanted."

"No sense worrying about it now, Gordo." Donny got to his feet. "Mama did what she did, Grandma did what she did, and that's that."

I watched him walk to the door. With his hand on the knob, he looked back at Mrs. Sullivan. "You got any idea how long it will be before the estate's settled?"

Donny spoke like he didn't especially care, it wasn't really important, but he didn't fool me. I knew darn well my brother could hardly wait to take his share of Grandma's money out to Tulsa and throw it all away gambling and drinking. It made me sick, but I didn't say anything. Like he'd just said—he'd do what he'd do, and that was that.

"At least two or three months," Mrs. Sullivan said. Something cold in her voice told me Donny hadn't fooled her either.

Donny nodded and slid out the door like he was oiled. The silence he left behind was broken only by the *ratcheta ratcheta ratcheta* of the Ford's engine cranking slowly to life.

After we went to bed that night, William and I lay awake talking for a long time. Since June and I were leaving the next day, we had lots to say to each other, but we started out with ordinary stuff—baseball, football, and the row of brand-new television sets we'd seen lined up in the Pep Boys' store window. Nobody we knew had a television yet, so the only way to watch stuff like horse races and wrestling matches was to stand on the sidewalk outside the shop and stare through the glass.

I'd tried to interest Grandma in buying a television, but she'd said she had better things to do than watch fat men jump up and down on each other. William hadn't had any luck with his mother, either.

Next William brought up his uncle Pete's new Studebaker. "It's the neatest car," he said. "Sleek and modern as all get-out. It makes Fords and Plymouths look like old-lady cars. And the engine's so quiet—just like a cat purring."

"Donny's worked on lots of cars," I said, "and he says nothing can beat a Buick."

After that there was nothing to talk about but the thing we'd been avoiding all night.

"I wish you weren't leaving tomorrow," William said softly.

"Me, too."

"I'm really going to miss you."

"I'll miss you, too, William."

"No, you won't," he said, getting mad all of a sudden. "You'll go back to College Hill and forget all about me. I'll just be this dumb old crippled kid you knew down in North Carolina."

"William, you do beat all," I said. "You walk so good now, hardly anyone would guess you wear a built-up shoe. And you're far from dumb. If I had half your brains, I'd be dangerous."

"Yeah, yeah," William muttered, "but what about your old friends? You'll meet up with them and never give me a thought."

"How many times have I told you I have exactly two friends in College Hill? Toad Sutcliffe and Doug Murray. For all I know, they've moved away by now. They could be jerks, they could be boring, they could even be in reform school. Maybe I'll hate them, maybe they'll hate me."

I inched farther over the edge of the bunk to see William better. He was squinting up at me, his eyes big and soft without his glasses. "Maybe you're the one who'll forget me," I said. "Did you ever think of that?"

"Don't be stupid, Gordy. Every time I look next door, I'll think about you not being there anymore."

"Suppose a family moves into Grandma's house," I said, though it pained me to picture such a thing, "and they have a kid our age and you get to be friends with him. Suppose he's smart like you, suppose your mother likes him better than me—which won't be hard. Pretty soon you won't even remember my name. Smith—easy to forget."

I don't know how long we would have argued if Mrs. Sullivan hadn't come to the door and told us to go to sleep. "You have to get up early tomorrow," she reminded us.

After his mother left, William said, "I bet you won't write me one measly little letter. Not even a postcard."

"You know how hard writing is for me," I said. "It makes my hand hurt, plus it wearies my brain."

"I'll write to you," William muttered. "Whether you write to me or not."

"Okay, okay," I grumbled. "I'll write—but you better not make fun of my spelling or anything. It's not like you're the teacher. I don't want you giving me a grade."

That seemed to satisfy William. He gave a little grunt, turned over on his side, and fell asleep, leaving me lying there, wide-eyed in the dark. If William hadn't been sound asleep, I'd have leaned over the edge of the bunk and told him he was the only real friend I'd ever had. Toad and Doug didn't even come close.

The next morning, Mrs. Sullivan drove June, me, and William to the station. The sky was a dull gray, not much different from the way it was the day we'd arrived in Grandville two years ago. The cold, damp air stunk of old soot and cinders, damp wood, and something worse. Dog pee, maybe.

While Mrs. Sullivan entertained June, William and I

settled ourselves side by side on a baggage cart and waited for the northbound train. We didn't say much, just sat there swinging our legs and staring down the tracks. I guess we'd talked ourselves dry the night before.

William sighed loudly, and I chucked a stone at a crow hopping along the edge of the platform. I didn't try to hit him, but the stone came close enough to startle him. He flew a few feet farther down the platform and kept on hopping, looking for breakfast, probably.

"Where's Donny?" William asked. "I thought he'd be here."

I spit hard. "He was probably out all night raising hell. Now he's sleeping it off."

William gave me a shrewd look. There was no fooling him. He knew I cared more than I was letting on. But he had the sense not to call me on it.

Just as I was about to give up hope, Donny's old Ford rounded the corner and screeched to a stop, spraying cinders and gravel. June ran to meet him. I watched him swing her up in the air.

"I'm going to miss you, June Bug," he said.

"How about me?" I asked. "Are you going to miss me, too?"

"Miss that ugly mug of yours? Are you crazy?"

For a second I thought Donny was serious, but he grabbed me in a half nelson and roughed me around. "Of course I'll miss you, you little twerp."

June hung on Donny. "I wish you were coming on the train with us."

"You have Gordy to look after you," he said. "And Stu. You don't need me."

June held him tighter, her face scrunched like she had a bellyache. "Will you send me a postcard from Oklahoma?"

"Sure thing, June, sure thing." Donny grinned down at her, and I hoped he was telling the truth. We'd already lost Mama and the little boys. I didn't want to lose Donny, too.

"You better send us your address," I told him.

Just as Donny opened his mouth to answer, the train came thundering into sight, puffing a cloud of smoke as gray as the sky. Its whistle drowned out every word he spoke. June put her fingers in her ears and drew closer to Mrs. Sullivan.

Silently we watched the locomotive slow to a stop. The conductor hopped off and helped an old lady down from a car. A man with a briefcase hurried past like he had important business in Grandville. A couple of women followed him, chattering and laughing.

"All aboard," the conductor hollered, looking straight at us.

I picked up my suitcase and shook William's hand. Like June, he had tears in his eyes. Or maybe it was just a cinder.

"Don't forget to write," he said. "You promised, Gordy."

Mrs. Sullivan put June's hand in mine. "Take care of your sister. Make sure she doesn't talk to strangers. Don't you talk to them, either. Even if they offer you candy."

Donny laughed. "Fat chance anybody would offer Gordy candy—he'd never be that lucky."

Mrs. Sullivan nudged us toward the train. The conductor helped June into the passenger car, and I struggled up the steps behind them, lugging both suitcases. As soon as we found a seat, we pressed our faces against the window and waved. Donny leaned against the baggage cart, a cigarette dangling old man–style from his lower lip. Mrs. Sullivan stood beside him, her hair blowing, one hand clutching her purse and the other raised in farewell. As the train began to move, William hobbled along beside us, shouting things I couldn't hear.

Suddenly the train picked up speed and William dropped out of sight. I got a glimpse of the Winn Dixie where Grandma used to shop, the Amoco station where Donny worked, the boardinghouse where he lived, the elementary school, a church or two, and, high on a hill just outside town, the cemetery.

Then, like a magician's trick, Grandville was gone. Fields and farms streaked past. Brown land under a gray sky. No color anywhere.

Like it or not, I was on my way back to College Hill.

4

It was a long ride to College Hill. I spent the first part of it trying to explain things to June. She didn't remember much about Stu or Barbara or Barbara's little boy, Brent, so it was up to me to fill her in on the details.

"Stu's nice," I started, "but he's kind of a chump. He deserted from the army during the war, and he—"

"The big war with Hitler? The one Donny went to?"

I nodded. "Stu didn't think it was right to kill, no matter what, so he—"

"That's in the Bible," June interrupted. "Thou shalt not kill. We learned it in Sunday school."

"Well, it's different in a war," I said. "It's okay to kill your enemy then."

"But—"

"Will you quit interrupting and let me finish what I'm trying to tell you?"

June's face puckered like she was going to cry,

but at least she shut her mouth for a few seconds.

"After Stu deserted," I went on," me and my friends, Toad and Doug, hid him in a hut we built in the woods, but he got sick and these two nosy girls, Lizard and Magpie, found out and tried to help."

June giggled. "Lizard and Magpie? Are they really named that?"

"Well, no, that's just what I call them. They—"

"What are their real names?"

I sighed. "Elizabeth Crawford and Margaret Baker. Now will you hush?"

June's lip jutted out, but she settled down again and let me talk.

"It was Magpie's idea to drag Barbara into it," I said. "Barbara was married to this guy who was killed in the war, so I thought she'd hate Stu for deserting, but she'd known him ever since they were little and she'd always liked him a lot. She ended up taking him to her house. He got better and then—"

"I remember what happened next," June said, sliding closer to me. "Daddy started whipping us and Stu came home and tried to make him stop and Daddy hit him so hard Stu had to go to the hospital."

"And the old man went to jail." That day wasn't something I liked to think about, and I was sorry June remembered it.

"But now Daddy's in California with Mama and Victor and Ernie and Bobby." June's voice sank a little lower. "And they're never coming back."

"And Stu's married to Barbara," I said, trying to make the ending sound happy.

June's eyes filled with worry shadows. "Will we like living with Stu and Barbara?"

"Sure we will, June Bug," I said, hoping I was telling her the truth.

June sighed. "I miss Grandma so much," she whispered. "I just don't think I'll be happy anywhere again, ever in my whole life. Not without her."

I blinked, swallowed hard, and patted June's bony little shoulder. I wanted to comfort her, but I didn't know what to tell her. I'd never been good with words. Whenever I tried to say the right thing, I always ended up making matters worse. So I just kept on patting her shoulder.

"Why did Grandma have to die?" June asked. "It's not fair, Gordy, it's not fair."

She'd begun to cry, so I put my arm around her. "Nothing's fair," I muttered. "Not life, not anything."

What I'd said was true, but as usual I'd failed to make June feel one bit better. She flung herself against me, crying in earnest. I stroked her hair and let her cry until she finally fell asleep. A big help I was.

While June slept, I stared out the train window. The glass was dirty and streaked with rain, but it didn't matter. There was nothing to see. I kept on looking, though, as if I expected to glimpse something that might explain my life—maybe a billboard with a message written in huge letters just for me.

Like I'd told June, life wasn't fair. As soon as you thought you were safe, somebody pulled the rug out from under you. And there you were, back on the train, going to the very place you thought you'd left for good.

5

Stu was the first person I saw when I got off the train. I'd thought married life would fatten him up, but he was just as skinny as I remembered. Still pale, still kind of sorrowful, he wore faded jeans and a scuffed-up leather jacket a little short in the sleeves.

Stu's face brightened when he saw June and me. He rushed forward and gave me a hug. "It's great to see you, Gordy. And you, too, June Bug!" He swung June up in the air, letting her long legs dangle.

Barbara popped out from behind Stu, smiling and pulling Brent forward to say hello. Her dark hair shone in the cold January sunlight, and her cheeks were as rosy as Brent's. She hadn't changed either. I hoped Stu knew how lucky he was to be married to such a good-looking dame.

"Gordy, just look at you!" Barbara cried. "When did you get so handsome?"

Too embarrassed to answer, I pulled away from her. Me handsome—what a laugh.

"And June," Barbara went on, "you've grown at least four inches!"

While Barbara fussed over June, I glanced at Brent. He didn't return my smile—just scowled like he'd heard all about me and had no plans to be friends. The last time I'd seen him, he was just starting to walk. Now he had the look of a real pest. Probably spoiled rotten, too.

Stu led us across the train tracks to a ramshackle old wooden apartment house. I'd known a kid who lived there when we were in second grade. He was the only boy in College Hill who knew more cuss words than I did, but he moved before I learned them all. Didn't even say good-bye—his family packed up and left town in the middle of the night without paying two or three months' rent. His old man wasn't any better than mine.

The place looked even worse than I remembered—peeling paint, sagging porch, scraggly bushes full of tattered newspapers and other trash, dingy wash hanging from sagging clotheslines. On one side was a cinder parking lot occupied by an ancient black Ford and a Chevy so faded I couldn't guess its color. On the other, a muddy creek ran along between weedy banks.

I might have known Stu would end up in the only dump in College Hill worse than our old house on Davis Road.

Inside, the stairs leading to the third floor were steep

and narrow, and the air smelled like other people's dinners. I heard at least three radios, all playing the same soap opera, a baby crying, a dog barking, and a man and woman arguing.

The apartment was smaller than I'd expected—three dinky little rooms plus a kitchen, a bathroom, and a tiny alcove just big enough for June's bed. It was fixed up nice, though—pictures on the walls, rugs, comfortable furniture, and a table big enough for five if you didn't mind being poked by your neighbor's elbow.

Before we'd even taken off our coats, Brent pointed to a box of toys in the corner—trucks and cars, blocks, a big red ball, and a mangy teddy bear without eyes. "Mine," he yelled. "Mine. My bear, my tucks, my tars, my ball, my bocks—MINE!"

While Brent hollered, June stared at Barbara with those big puppy-dog eyes, just begging her to like her. If somebody didn't say something to her soon, she'd start crying.

Finally Barbara noticed and gave June a hug. "Stu, show Gordy where to put his things," she said. "I'll help June get settled. The poor child's exhausted."

Stu led me to Brent's room. His bed was in one corner, my bed in the other, so close we could hold hands all night without even stretching. Between the beds was a little bookcase crammed with Brent's books. Against one wall was a bureau. Barbara had cleaned out two drawers for me. And half a tiny closet. It was lucky I didn't have a lot of stuff.

"I'm sorry you can't have a room of your own," Stu said. "Even with me working part-time, it's hard to pay the rent."

"You'll be getting some money from Grandma one of these days," I said. "Maybe you can use it to buy a house."

"That's what Barbara's hoping." Stu didn't seem to be expecting it to happen anytime soon. For now I'd have to put up with sharing a room with Brent, who was giving me an ugly look.

After Stu left, I opened my suitcase and started to unpack. Brent thrust himself between me and the bureau. "My room," he shouted. "My burro!" Grabbing a pair of my socks, he threw them on the floor and scowled at me.

"Pick those up," I told him. "You're bunking with me now, kid. Don't get too big for your britches."

Instead of doing what I told him, Brent threw another pair of socks on the floor. "Big poopoo head!" he bellowed.

For a second I considered giving him a whack he'd remember. In fact, my hand was up and moving toward his face like it had a life of its own, but I stopped myself just in time. No sense making everybody mad at me right off the bat.

"Poopoo head yourself," I said, dumping my socks in the drawer and slamming it shut.

Brent glared at me, red in the face and not the slightest bit scared. "Dumb peepee pig."

"Brent!" Barbara ran into the room and pulled my

little roommate away from the bureau. "What did Mommy tell you? You have to share with Uncle Gordy now."

Uncle Gordy? I stared at Barbara, too surprised to say a word. Till then, I hadn't given any thought to my exact relationship to Brent. Since we weren't blood kin, I guessed I was his step-uncle—if there was such a thing.

"Yuncle Poopoo," Brent muttered.

As Barbara led the brat away, he stuck his tongue out at me. I stuck mine out, too—even though it wasn't a very dignified thing for an uncle to do. Then I went back to putting my clothes away.

By dinnertime, Brent had raided the bureau twice and dumped all my socks in the toilet. He was caught when he tried to flush them down, stopped up the toilet, and flooded the bathroom floor.

When June saw my socks, she laughed so hard she almost wet her pants, but Barbara didn't seem to find it very funny. She was juggling pots and pans, burning the potatoes by the smell of it, and trying to keep an eye on Brent.

"Poor Uncle Gordy," Stu said, hanging my socks over the shower rod to dry.

"Bad Yuncle Poopoo," said Brent, which made Auntie June laugh again. It looked like she and Brent were going to get along just swell.

At the table, Brent entertained us by mashing his

peas into his potatoes and eating them with his fingers. When Barbara told him to stop playing with his food, he rolled his bread into little balls and threw them at me. Then he spilled his milk so it ran into my lap. From the way he grinned, I swear he did it on purpose. It was like living with a three-foot-high troll.

Between June giggling at everything the troll did and Barbara saying, "Brent, sit up straight and behave," I got a bellyache so bad I had to lie down on the sofa.

"It's probably gas" was all Barbara had to say.

After June and Brent went to bed, I started to feel better. Peace and quiet were definitely good for bellyaches. Not that it lasted long. I'd just gotten interested in *Gangbusters,* one of my favorite radio shows, when Barbara set up a typewriter on the table and started pounding the keys.

"Do you have to do that now?" I asked. "I'm trying to listen to the radio."

"See this?" Barbara pointed at a stack of paper. "I promised I'd have it typed tomorrow."

"What is it?"

"A thesis on cattle diseases."

"I didn't know you were interested in stuff like that." I started to laugh. "Are you planning to be a farmer?"

She didn't laugh. "I'm typing it for a graduate student, Gordy."

Stu gave her a hug. "Barb brings in half our income typing," he said. "She's fast, she's accurate, and she knows how to spell."

Barbara smiled at Stu. "They call me the fastest gun on campus," she said, and went back to typing.

Stu kissed the top of her head and turned to me. "You ought to go to bed soon anyway, Gordy. School starts at nine, but we'll have to leave early so I won't be late for work."

"School?" I stared at Stu, stunned. "Can't I have a couple of days to get used to being here first?"

Stu shook his head. "Education's important. I don't want you to miss anything."

"But, Stu—"

"We'll take the streetcar around eight," he went on, sounding a lot bossier than I remembered. "That should give me plenty of time to get to the cabinet shop."

I slumped on the sofa, too depressed to argue. School—that meant Toad and Doug, Lizard, Magpie, and a bunch of other creeps and jerks I'd left behind two years ago, hoping never to see them again. "Did you tell anybody I was coming back?" I asked.

"Just Elizabeth Crawford and Margaret Baker," Stu said. "They baby-sit for Brent a couple of days a week so Barbara can get some typing done. Do you remember them?"

I groaned. "You'll probably have to find a new baby sitter. Those girls won't come near this place if they know I'm here. They hate my guts."

Stu grinned. "They giggled and made a few wisecracks, but they didn't say anything about quitting. As a matter of fact, I have a feeling they'll be looking for you at school."

I wasn't sure how to interpret that, but I decided I'd keep an eye out for Lizard and Magpie, too. There was no telling what they'd planned to celebrate my return—a big pot of boiling oil, a shotgun, tar and feathers.

"Wait till you see Elizabeth," Stu went on. "She must be the prettiest girl in College Hill."

"Lizard's not so hot," I muttered. "She's got a chicken pox scar on her cheek, for one thing. Plus she's bossy. Stuck-up, too."

I went on and on, telling Stu all the things that were wrong with Lizard. "Any boy who fell for her would have to be a moron," I concluded.

Stu laughed. "You beat everything, Gordy."

"You better believe it." Tired of talking, I heaved myself off the couch and said good night. If I was going to school tomorrow, I'd better get my beauty sleep.

After I brushed my teeth, I tiptoed into Brent's room, undressed, and crawled into bed, praying the troll wouldn't wake up and start hollering.

The kid didn't make a sound, but I lay awake, tossing and turning till way after midnight. I swear I heard every train that roared past, whistles blowing, engines rumbling, crossing bells ringing. My bed shook. The windowpanes rattled. It was as bad as our old house on Davis Road.

Worse yet, people tramped back and forth upstairs, making so much noise it sounded like they were wearing combat boots and dropping barbells on the floor. Next door, someone coughed every few minutes. Must have had TB or something. A radio played so loud I could recognize Hank Williams singing "Your Cheatin' Heart." Dogs barked. The fire siren went off, and the dogs howled—which made barking seem good.

But it wasn't just the noise that kept me awake. It was lonesomeness—no Grandma sleeping down the hall from me, no William next door, no Donny to cadge Cokes from at the Amoco station. When the sun came up, I'd look out the window and see College Hill—the place I got my miserable start in life.

At least the old man was far away—but not forgotten. No, sir. Not by me or anyone else.

6

TRUE TO HIS WORD, STU GOT ME UP BRIGHT AND EARLY. Even though elementary school didn't start till nine o'clock, June was already sitting at the breakfast table, bright-eyed and ready to go.

"Do I look all right, Gordy?" She smoothed her dress. "Barbara French braided my hair—isn't it pretty? She says Miss Porter will be my teacher. Did you have her in third grade?"

When June paused to take a sip of orange juice, I told her she looked nice, her braids were pretty, and no, I'd never heard of Miss Porter. She must be new—which was a good thing. If June ever had a teacher who remembered me, she'd be in big trouble. I didn't tell her that, of course. No sense giving the poor kid something else to worry about.

"I want to go tool too," the troll yelled. When nobody said anything, he knocked over his orange juice. This time I saw it coming and got out of the way fast.

"Eat up, Gordy," Stu said. "We have to be on the streetcar by eight."

I choked down the rest of my lumpy oatmeal and gulped a glass of milk. After Stu gave Barbara a hug and a kiss, I followed him outside. Another cold, gray day. I swear the sun hadn't shone since Grandma died. Maybe it never would. Winter would just go on and on.

I half expected, half dreaded seeing someone I knew, but, except for a mean-eyed dog peeing on a telephone pole, the streetcar stop was deserted. Maybe it was too early for any of my old acquaintances to be out.

Stu and I waited side by side, shivering in the wind. The two of us had never had much to talk about, probably because we were too different. I'd always been closer to Donny—it was easier for me to imagine blowing up toilets than deserting from the army.

Suddenly Stu put his hand on my shoulder. "I saw your report cards from Grandville, Gordy. Lots of Bs, even a few As. Promise me you'll keep up the good work here."

I didn't answer, didn't even look at him, just spit on the streetcar track. If it had been summer, it would have sizzled when it hit the hot metal, but today it just lay there, a slimy gray blob about the size of a quarter.

Stu squeezed my shoulder. "Try," he said. "That's all I'm asking."

"Yeah, sure, okay," I muttered.

The streetcar swung into sight then, and Stu got busy counting out the change we'd need for the fare. I glanced at him just long enough to see the familiar sad look on his face. He, June, and Mama had definitely been cut from the same cloth.

A few minutes later, the streetcar slowed for Garfield Road. Lizard and Magpie lived down at the end of the street near the train tracks, but I didn't see them anywhere. Not that I wanted to. What a pair they were—dumbest girls I'd ever known.

A few seconds later, we passed the house where Barbara lived before she married Stu.

"Do Barbara's folks still live there?" I asked Stu.

He shook his head. "They moved to Florida last year, after her dad retired."

"Too bad they didn't give you the house," I said, remembering the nice big rooms.

Stu shrugged. "They needed to sell it to buy the new place in Florida."

I looked at him. "What did they think of you and Barbara getting hitched?"

Stu's face got so long I wondered if Barbara had been disowned. I once saw a western movie about a rich girl who married a poor cowboy and got kicked out by her father. Later the cowboy saved the father's ranch and the daughter was forgiven. Movies always had happy endings, but real life hardly ever did.

"I guess they'd have liked it better if I'd had a good job," Stu said finally, "but we get along all right." He sighed and looked out the window.

Ten minutes later, we got off the streetcar and walked a few blocks to the school. Hyattsdale was a big old rambling brick building, at least twice the size of Grandville High. The main part was so ancient, I knew kids whose parents had gone there, but it had been added on to over the years.

One wing was three stories high. If you had a class on a lower floor, Donny said you could see up the girls' skirts as they came down the fire escape from the third floor during fire drills. That was the only good thing he had to say about the place. With my luck there wouldn't be any fire drills when I was on a lower floor.

School hadn't started, so the hall was empty. The still air reeked of chalk dust, paper, pencil shavings, oiled wood floors, and old spaghetti sauce. Under everything else, there was a faint stink of pee from the radiators in the boys' room.

In the office, Stu told the school secretary I was a new eighth grader. Laying down her pen with a sigh, she led us to the principal's door.

"Mr. Mueller?" The secretary practically trembled when Mueller raised his head and scowled at her. "I hate to bother you, sir, but we have a new student."

"Send him in." Mueller's voice was gruff. Under a mop of white hair, his face was deeply creased, especially around the corners of his mouth. No smile lines—but plenty of frown lines.

Stu offered his hand politely and introduced us. "You probably don't remember me, sir," he added, "but I graduated in 1943, and our brother Donny finished in '41."

"Stuart and Donald Smith?" The creases in Mr. Mueller's face got even deeper. "Yes, I remember you," he said, "and your brother, too. I believe Donald spent more time in my office than any student in the history of this school. Played hooky, flunked almost every course, got himself arrested for blowing up a toilet at the Esso station with a firecracker, and did not graduate in 1941—or ever."

Stu must have been just as mad as I was, but he didn't say a word in Donny's defense. All he did was shove his hands into his pockets and study the floor as if something interesting was taking place there. I felt like walking out, but I knew that would upset Stu, so I stayed where I was, lounging against the door frame and scowling. No sense letting Mueller think I was a chump, too.

Stu handed Mueller the envelope my old principal in Grandville had given me. "Please register Gordy," he said. "I'm late for work already."

As Mueller perused my grades, his eyebrows rose. "Well, except for math, you appear to be a fairly decent student, Gordon."

I kept on scowling. Somehow Mueller made my grades seem worthless, nothing to brag about, barely adequate. Except for that D in algebra, Grandma had been proud of my report card. If she'd been with me, she wouldn't have kowtowed to Mueller like Stu. No, sir, she'd have given him a piece of her mind he wouldn't soon forget.

"You'll find the work more difficult here," Mueller went on. "It's a known fact that southern schools are way behind ours."

"I'm sure Gordy won't have any trouble meeting your standards," Stu said. For him that was tough talk.

Without looking up from the forms he was filling out, Mueller nodded. "You may go now, Stuart. I'll make sure Gordon gets to his first class."

After Stu left, Mueller leaned back in his chair and studied me for a long minute, taking in every detail of my appearance like he was memorizing me. "Stuart was a good student," he said. "Graduated at the top of his class and won a full scholarship to the University of Maryland. Then he was drafted. When he deserted, he disappointed me. I had high hopes for that boy."

I looked Mueller in the eye. "Stu's doing okay. He's in college now, studying to be an English teacher." As I spoke, I felt my face heat with shame. It seemed to me I'd been defending Stu long enough. He should have taken up for himself once in a while, but he never did.

Mueller cleared his throat and went on talking as if I hadn't said a thing. "On the other hand, Donald dropped out of school the day he turned sixteen. Believe me, I wasn't a bit sorry to lose *him*." He paused and gave me another long hard look. "I wonder which of your brothers you take after, Gordon."

It was just the way I'd known it would be—everybody remembered my father and my brothers. They all expected me to turn out every bit as bad as they had. The only question was, whose path would I follow? Would I become the town drunk? Would I drop out of school and blow up gas stations? Would I desert if another war started?

When I didn't say anything, Mueller frowned. "I plan to keep an eye on you, Gordon. Any sign of misbehavior and I'll come down on you hard. Is that clear?"

"Yes, sir," I muttered. His message was clear. It was my first day at Hyattsdale High, and the principal already hated me.

With that, Mueller turned me over to Miss Greenbaum, the school secretary. She adjusted her glasses, smoothed her skirt, and led me down the hall to my first class—English with Mrs. Ianotti.

7

It wasn't till lunchtime that I saw anybody I knew, except for a couple of snobby girls I'd always hated. They didn't seem to remember me, which was just as well. The second I stepped into the cafeteria, though, Doug and Toad spotted me. Toad was fatter than ever and at least two inches taller than I was. Doug had shot up about a foot, and his voice was starting to change, which put him ahead of me in both departments.

Down in North Carolina I hadn't noticed how short I was—after all, I was taller than William. But here in Maryland I felt like a shrimp. Maybe it was because I used to be bigger than either Toad or Doug and now I wasn't. Whatever the reason, it didn't make me feel good to look up to guys I used to lead around by the nose—to borrow one of Doug's mother's favorite expressions.

"It's great to see you, Gordy!" Toad slung his arm around my shoulders and led me toward a table in the corner. "We heard you were coming back."

"Yeah, your old girlfriend told us." Doug whistled. "You seen Crawford yet?"

I shook my head. "She's not my girlfriend. Never was, never will be." All the time I was saying this, I was trying not to look around the cafeteria for Lizard. Though it didn't make much sense, I wanted to see her but I didn't want anybody to see me seeing her, including Lizard herself.

"There she is." Toad pointed across the room.

That gave me an excuse to turn around and stare. Lizard was standing in the lunch line, talking to Magpie, giggling about something. Seeing her had a terrible effect on my heart. It even affected my breathing. If I'd had to say something at that moment, I'd have choked.

Luckily Toad was too busy leering at Lizard to notice the effect she was having on me. "How'd you like to get her in the back row of the Hyattsdale Movie Theater?"

"Hoo boy," said Doug, eyeing Lizard's blue sweater.

"Trouble is, she has a zillion boyfriends." Toad sighed and bit into his apple, spraying juice all over my cheek.

While Toad and Doug went on talking, I stared at Lizard. She was even prettier than I remembered. Much prettier. Gorgeous, in fact. Her hair was long and blond and shiny. Every time she moved her head, it swirled around her face. I wished I was standing close enough for it to brush my cheek. It would smell sweet, I thought, and feel as tickly as feathers.

Best of all, Lizard was way shorter than Magpie—which meant she was probably about my height.

Poor old Magpie was not only tall but also just as skinny and freckled as ever. She'd cut off her braids, and her brown hair hung to her shoulders in what June called a pageboy. She was wearing horn-rimmed glasses, which gave her a brainy look.

All of a sudden Lizard turned her head and saw me. For a second our eyes locked like we were enchanted or something. I gave her a Humphrey Bogart grin, the kind dames go for in the movies, but I must not have gotten it right because she grabbed Magpie and pointed at me. Then they both started laughing. Not just giggling, but howling like they'd never seen anybody as funny as me.

Luckily neither Toad nor Doug noticed. While I'd been gawking at stuck-up Lizzy Lizard, they'd started talking about the school basketball game coming up this weekend.

"The Hawks haven't got a chance against the Mustangs," Toad said. "They'll walk all over us."

"Bet you a quarter we win," Doug said.

"Done." Toad turned to me. "How about you, Gordy? Want to bet whether we win or lose?"

I shrugged. What did I care about Hawks and Mustangs?

There was a little silence. Toad and Doug glanced at each other, and then Doug leaned across the table. "Lizard told us about your grandmother, Gordy. I guess you're still feeling kind of down in the dumps about it."

He sounded embarrassed, as if mentioning death

was bad manners or something. Beside him, Toad nodded to show he was sorry too but not up to actually saying it. They both looked so uncomfortable, I felt like I should apologize for losing Grandma.

Instead I sucked up the rest of my milk and got to my feet. "Let's go," I said. "It's hot in here."

Though I didn't plan to look at Lizard again, I passed right by her table. She and Magpie were sitting with three other girls I vaguely remembered from grade school. Luckily they were too busy talking to notice me.

After school, Toad, Doug, and I strolled down Oglethorpe Street toward the streetcar stop. Just ahead of us, I spotted Lizard, Magpie, and Polly Anderson. Without thinking, I picked up a stone, just a little one, and tossed it at Lizard. It hit her in the back, and, even though it couldn't have hurt her, she whirled around like I'd thrown a rock the size of a baseball at her.

"Boy, you haven't changed a bit, Gordy Smith!" she hollered. "You're just the same as ever—rude and ugly and dumb."

Magpie and Polly huddled together like they thought I meant to stone them to death. I'd only been fooling around. Couldn't they see that?

"Neither have you, Lizard," I sneered. "You're the same little snot you always were."

But I was lying. Not about her being a snot. Lizard

was definitely the same in that category. But she hadn't bothered to button her coat, and I could see the changes in her shape I'd noticed in the cafeteria.

Unfortunately, she realized what I was looking at and pulled her coat shut. "Why did you have to come back?" she asked. "We were getting along just fine without you!"

Without saying another word, she walked away with Magpie and Polly.

I yelled a few insults at her, but she just walked faster. Not that I cared. She made me sick.

We all ended up on the same streetcar, but the girls sat in the front and never looked at us once, not even when I hit Lizard's cheek with a spitball. I watched her and Magpie get off at Garfield Road, thinking I might follow them, but Toad wanted to treat me to a soda at the Trolley Stoppe Shoppe to celebrate my return. I couldn't turn that down. So I rode two stops more and got off at College Avenue.

The three of us pushed open the Trolley Stoppe Shoppe's double doors like outlaws entering an old-time saloon and grabbed seats at the counter.

"Look." I pointed to the initials I'd carved into the wood way back in sixth grade. "They're still here."

"Yeah, but did you see this?" Toad directed my attention to a change I hadn't noticed. "'G.A.S. *stinks.*'"

Doug started to laugh. "By golly, gas does stink."

That set Toad off, but I just sat there, staring at the counter. Though I'd carved *G.P.S.*—Gordon Peter Smith

—somebody had changed the *P* to an *A* and added *stinks*. For some reason I was sure Lizard had done it. It was just the kind of thing she'd think was funny.

"Well, what'll you have, Gordo?" Toad asked, trying to jolly me up.

I scowled at him to show what I thought of all that stupid hee-hawing at my expense. "A cherry Coke," I muttered. "And make it large. I'm thirsty."

While I waited for my drink, I got a pencil and started scratching out *G.A.S. stinks*. It wasn't easy. Both Lizard and I had dug deep into the wood. While I worked, I asked Toad and Doug what they'd been doing lately.

Doug spun around on his stool and shrugged. "Not much."

"Life just hasn't been the same without you, Gordo," Toad said.

"Yeah," Doug agreed. "Me and Toad tried a few stunts —stealing stuff from the variety store, playing hooky, putting garbage cans on the trolley tracks. But we always got caught."

The guy behind the counter set three glasses in front of us. "One large vanilla, one cherry, and one chocolate," he said. "That'll be thirty cents, gentlemen."

Toad handed him the money and grabbed his chocolate Coke. I took mine and slid the vanilla down the counter toward Doug the way they do in western movies.

"How about our old hut in the woods?" I asked. "Do you ever go there anymore?"

Doug and Toad exchanged looks. "We had a little

accident—" Toad began and then stopped, like he was too embarrassed to go on.

"With the lantern," Doug added, equally embarrassed.

"What happened?"

Toad's face turned scarlet. "We knocked it over."

"Burned the whole thing to the ground," Doug said.

"You burned my hut down?" I stared at the two of them, more upset than I cared to admit. Before I'd fallen asleep the night before, I'd been thinking about living there in my own private wilderness, trapping and hunting, catching my own food, living like somebody in a Jack London story. Rabbits, squirrels, muskrats—anything would be better than eating with the troll every night. Now I had nowhere to go unless I wanted to build the whole thing over again. Which I didn't.

"It wasn't just the hut that burned," Toad went on. "The woods caught fire, too."

"Fire engines came from everywhere—College Hill, Riverside, Berwyn Heights." Doug started laughing. "It was really something."

Forgetting to be embarrassed, Toad laughed too. "It was like that lady in Chicago and her cow," he said. "You just wouldn't believe how fast that fire spread."

"We tried to put it out," Doug began, but Toad interrupted.

"That's how we got caught," he said, so excited he sprayed me with spit. "The firemen saw us, and somehow or other, I'm still not sure how, they realized we'd started it."

"We thought we'd be sent to reform school for sure," Doug said, "but my dad hired a good lawyer." He sucked the last of his Coke through his straw with a loud slurp. "After that, he and Mom started talking about military academies."

There was a little silence. A college girl dropped a nickel into the jukebox, and Frank Sinatra's voice came floating out, singing "All or Nothing at All." The college girl and her friends all swooned against each other like they might drop dead at the sound of Frankie's voice. Silly dames.

"So what are we going to do now that you're back?" Toad spun round and round on his stool, grinning at me like a good-natured dog.

I guessed he was hoping I'd come up with an exciting idea, but nothing occurred to me. I was too depressed about the hut. "What do you guys want to do?" I asked.

Doug and Toad both spun around on their stools. "Don't know," Toad said.

Doug looked at his watch. "Hey, I better get going," he said. "I've got a ton of homework to do."

"Yeah, me, too." Toad slid off his stool. "How about you, Gordy? You got any homework?"

Doug laughed. "Wise up, Toad. Gordy never does homework. He doesn't have to. Even if he was dumber than dirt, teachers would pass him to the next grade just to get rid of him."

I laughed and swaggered out of the Trolley Stoppe Shoppe, playing the part they expected me to play, but I was as mad as a bear with a sore behind. I was no genius, but I wasn't as dumb as Doug and Toad thought I was.

The three of us split up at Calvert Road, Toad heading for his house and Doug for his. "See you at the trolley stop tomorrow," Toad yelled from half a block away. "Eight-fifteen. Okay?"

I waved to show I'd heard and walked down Calvert, taking in the familiar sights—my old elementary school, the creek I used to play in, trees I'd climbed, streetlights I'd busted, sidewalks I'd written cuss words on.

Nothing was quite the way I remembered it. The town seemed smaller, for one thing. The houses weren't as big and fancy as I'd thought. Even the elementary school had shrunk. It wouldn't have surprised me if my old sixth grade teacher turned out to be no taller than the troll.

I'd changed too, but Toad and Doug sure hadn't noticed. Neither had Lizard. She'd said I was the same as ever—rude and ugly and dumb. Her exact words.

It was enough to make me cuss out loud.

8

Halfway down Calvert Road, I saw Lizard and Magpie walking toward me, each holding one of the troll's grubby little hands. June was swinging Lizard's free hand and telling her something. She was the only one who looked happy to see me—which was no surprise.

"Gordy, Gordy," she yelled running toward me. "This is Elizabeth's and Margaret's day to baby-sit Brent. We're going to the playground. Want to come with us?"

I could have gone inside to listen to the radio or something, but that's just what Lizard and Magpie hoped I'd do. So I grabbed June's hand and grinned. "Sure, kiddo. Why not?"

"No Yuncle Poopoo!" the troll yelled, pushing me. "No Yuncle Poopoo!"

"Don't talk to Gordy like that," June said, but Lizard and Magpie practically had hysterics. You'd have thought the troll was Bob Hope and Red Skelton rolled into one big barrel of laughs.

"Yuncle Poopoo," Lizard cackled. "What a perfect name—it's even better than G.A.S."

I gave her an evil look, which she returned. It seemed I'd guessed right about who'd changed my initials at the Trolley Stoppe Shoppe. Turning to my sister, I asked her how school had been.

"Miss Porter says I'm a good artist and a good reader," June said, "but I'm way behind in arithmetic. They're doing division here already. We hadn't even started that in Grandville."

"Don't worry, June Bug. You're so smart, you'll catch up quick."

June frowned. "I hope so. I want to get gold stars like I did in Miss Trent's room."

With me trailing behind, June ran across the school playground, climbed to the top of the jungle gym, and hung upside down by her knees. "No hands," she yelled, stretching her palms out. "See?"

While June showed me her tricks, I watched Lizard push Brent higher and higher, running under the swing to make him laugh. She was wearing rolled-up jeans and a gray University of Maryland sweatshirt that must have belonged to her big brother, Joe. Unlike her blue sweater, it hid everything.

Lizard glanced my way and caught me staring at her. To my surprise, she handed Brent over to Magpie and, without actually looking at me, strolled toward the jungle gym. She stopped a couple of feet away and jammed her hands in her pockets. Meeting my eyes at last, she said, "I just want to say I'm sorry about your grandmother, Gordy. My grandmother passed away last summer, so I know how you feel."

I nodded, but I didn't say what I was thinking—which was that Lizard had a mother and a father and a nice house. She was smart and she was pretty. Everybody liked her. The little snot had no idea how I felt. Not even a clue.

Lizard waited a second like she thought I might say something. When I didn't, she ran back to the swings and started pushing Brent again.

As soon as she left, I felt like kicking myself for being such a dope. So Lizard didn't totally understand what it was like to lose Grandma—at least she'd said she was sorry. I could have been more friendly. Could at least have smiled. Now she'd probably never speak to me again.

Mad at the world, I climbed to the top of the jungle gym. The tall windows of my old sixth-grade classroom blazed in the light of the setting sun. From a block away, I heard the rumble of cars and trucks on Route 1. A man walked past, coming home from work, probably. A woman scurried along behind him, head down like she was scared of tripping on a crack in the sidewalk.

"Hey, June, it's time to go," Lizard yelled. She and Magpie were dragging Brent away from the swings. From the way he was howling, the troll must not have been ready to leave the playground.

I flipped off a high bar, a pretty good trick, but only June noticed. Lizard and Magpie were too busy with Brent to pay any attention to me.

By the time June and I caught up, Brent was walking between Lizard and Magpie, holding their hands. I could have walked faster and passed them, but I was enjoying the view of Lizard's hips and legs.

I felt like whistling, but instead I tried repeating something I'd heard Donny yell at girls. "Must be jelly," I shouted, "'cause jam don't shake like that."

Lizard turned and hollered, "Drop dead, Gordy!" Magpie gave me a dirty look, and Brent sang out, "Dumb old 'tupid Yuncle Poopoo!" Dragging the troll with them, the girls started running like they couldn't wait to get away from me.

Once again June and I tagged along behind the three of them. But I didn't enjoy the view as much as I had earlier. It seemed Lizard hated me more than ever. Just being near her put me in a lousy mood.

"What's wrong, Gordy?" June asked.

"Nothing." I must have said it louder than I meant to because June ran after Lizard and Magpie like I'd scared her away. I walked slower and slower, letting the distance widen until the four of them were no bigger than the dolls in June's dollhouse.

By the time I finally got to Stu's apartment, Lizard and Magpie were on their way down the stairs. When they saw me coming, they flattened themselves against the wall like I had cooties or something even worse—leprosy, maybe. I swear they held their breath to keep from inhaling my germs.

"It's been great seeing you two," I muttered.

"The pleasure was all *yours,*" Lizard said. Laughing like hyenas, she and Margaret ran outside.

I opened the apartment door and went straight to the bathroom. Turning on the water so people would think I was doing something legitimate, I stared out the window at the train tracks. A freight was coming, pulled by one of the new diesel engines. The boxcars thundered past, shaking the bathroom so hard that stuff in the medicine cabinet clinked.

Maybe I'd hop a freight and head west the way I'd always dreamed of doing. Jump off the train in Tulsa, find Donny, talk him into letting me stay with him. As soon as I turned sixteen, I'd drop out of school and get a job in the oil fields. By the time I was twenty-one, I'd be filthy rich.

I'd come back to College Hill driving a Cadillac convertible, top down. I'd stop for a traffic light on Route 1, and Lizard would walk across the road in front of me. She'd be so fat and ugly, I'd barely recognize her.

But she'd recognize me. "Oh, Gordy, it's great to see you," she'd gush. "I hear you're a millionaire ten times over now."

I'd sneer and gun the motor. "Believe me, the pleasure is all *yours,*" I'd say as I drove away.

I smiled at my reflection in the mirror. Wouldn't that fix Lizard's wagon?

9

A FEW DAYS LATER, TOAD AND DOUG AND I WERE SITTING at our table in the back of the cafeteria, gassing about basketball. While Doug gave a play-by-play account of the University of Maryland's big win over Duke, I sat there looking around the cafeteria, bored out of my mind. It wasn't that I hated basketball—I just didn't want to hear Doug describe every bounce of the ball.

Suddenly I spotted Lizard and Magpie in the lunch line. To my disgust, Lizard was talking to Bobby Pritchett, this kid I'd always hated, a stuck-up snob who lived in a big brick house at the top of Beech Drive. Like almost everybody else in College Hill, he'd grown. Though he used to be about my height, he was now almost as tall as Magpie. From the size of his shoulders, he might have been lifting weights while I was building model airplanes with William.

While I watched, hating him more every second,

Pritchett moved closer to Lizard till his face was about an inch from hers. I hoped his breath stunk.

Toad turned his head to see what I was looking at. "I hear Pritchett took Lizard to the movies last Saturday," he said.

"Why should I care who that little snot goes out with?" I asked. "I wouldn't take her around the block."

Doug gave me a look that said he didn't believe a word of it. "Pritchett plays JV basketball," he said. "He's been high scorer all season."

I scowled at Doug. "So what?"

"So he also played football last fall—first-string tackle," Toad put in, playing the loyal buddy role as usual. "All the girls are nuts about him."

"Including good old Lizard," Doug added.

"Hurray for her. Hurray for him, too." I crushed my empty milk carton in my fist the way Donny used to flatten beer cans and got to my feet.

"Where are you going?" Doug called after me.

Without bothering to answer, I swaggered over to the cooler and grabbed another carton of chocolate milk. Though I didn't plan it that way, I just happened to catch up with Pritchett. Somehow—I swear it was an accident—my foot got in front of his foot. The stupid idiot stumbled and bumped into Lizard. Her plate of spaghetti slid off her tray and hit the floor. Tomato sauce splattered everywhere, but most of it landed on Pritchett's trousers and Lizard's skirt.

"Look what you did, Gordy Smith!" Lizard yelled. "My skirt's ruined!"

Beside her, Magpie gripped her tray like she thought I might dump her spaghetti on the floor, too.

"Pritchett did that," I told Lizard. "If he'd been looking where he was going—"

"Don't blame me," Pritchett cut in before I'd finished. "You tripped me on purpose."

The jerk's size and height didn't scare me. Stepping right up to him, I gave him my best Bogart sneer and said, "It's not my fault you're blind in one eye and can't see out of the other."

Pritchett scowled. If he hadn't been holding a tray, he probably would have socked me—which would have given me the excuse I needed to punch his big ugly nose.

"I remember you," he said. "You used to live down at the end of Davis Road. Didn't one of your brothers desert or something?"

"So what if he did?" I would have hit Pritchett then, tray or no tray, but my shop teacher came up behind me, grabbed my shirt collar, and pulled me backward so hard I almost choked.

"What's going on here?" Mr. Boylan asked.

Pritchett pointed at the spaghetti sauce on the floor. "Gordon Smith tripped me, sir. He made me—"

"It was an *accident,*" I interrupted. "Pritchett wasn't looking where he was going. It's not my fault he—"

Boylan cut me off and turned to Lizard. "Did you see what happened?"

Lizard glanced at Pritchett. He smirked like he knew she'd defend him. Then she looked at me. I didn't waste my energy smiling. It was obvious whose side she was on.

"Gordy tripped Bobby," Lizard said, giving me the evil eye. "Maybe it was an accident, maybe it wasn't, but just look at my skirt. My mother's going to kill me when I get home."

Next Boylan asked Magpie what she'd seen. "I don't know," she whispered. "I wasn't looking, sir."

Boylan let go of my collar, shoving me a little at the same time. "Go sit down, Smith. If I catch you starting any more trouble, I'll send you to the office."

I strolled back to my seat, aware I had the whole cafeteria's attention. Toad and Doug gave me a big thumbs-up, and I bowed—Gordy Smith, spaghetti king.

After school, I saw Lizard at the streetcar stop. I would have said I was sorry about her skirt, but she was with Pritchett, smiling and laughing and tossing her stupid hair around. Why should I care what happened to her dumb old clothes?

When the streetcar came, I walked past Lizard without even looking at her and took a seat in the back with Toad and Doug. We laughed and shouted and pushed each other around till the driver threatened to throw us off. But Lizard never glanced my way, not once. She was laughing so hard at Pritchett's dumb jokes, the Russians could have dropped the A-bomb on Washington and she wouldn't have noticed.

If she'd only given me the chance, I could have told her some really good jokes, much better than Pritchett's. Thanks to William, I knew over a dozen Little Moron riddles. Donny had taught me a bunch of even funnier traveling salesman stories, but I couldn't tell her those—they were pretty dirty.

Pritchett rode right past his stop and got off the streetcar with Lizard and Magpie. I watched the three of them walk down Garfield toward Lizard's house. Lizard was still laughing at Pritchett's jokes—he must have had a million of them. But poor old Magpie trailed along behind, head down, clutching her notebook, looking as glum as I felt.

My stop was next. I didn't feel like hanging around with Toad and Doug or going home to Stu's, so I wandered around by myself, going up one street and down another, feeling lonesome and sad. The wind was blowing hard, and the sky was full of big dark clouds. Dead leaves tumbled every which way, some rushing ahead, some lagging behind, some spiraling into the air around me. The bare trees and brown grass made the whole town look ugly—houses, yards, garages, even telephone poles.

At the corner of Dartmoor and Davis Road, I stopped and looked down the street. Our old house was at the end. From where I stood, all I could see was the chimney and part of the roof, but being this close started a landslide of memories. My father sitting in his armchair by the radio, a bottle of beer in his hand, just waiting for somebody to give him an excuse to start punching us. Mama moving slow and quiet, speaking soft, hoping not to rile him. My little brothers playing in the yard, scared to come inside till the old man left—or passed out. June watching everything with those big sad puppy-dog eyes of hers. Donny blowing up toilets with cherry bombs. Stu down in the woods hiding from the war.

And me fighting, cussing, acting mean and hateful. Pulling Lizard's hair, calling her names, ruining her homework. No wonder she hated me.

Like a zombie controlled by forces too powerful to resist, I walked slowly down the street, half expecting to see the old black car parked in front of our house. It wasn't there, but for a second I thought I heard Victor yelling. When I got closer, I saw some other kid, a boy about my little brother's age, playing cowboys with two girls.

I'd expected the house to be an empty, falling-down wreck, everything busted and broken and dirty the way we'd left it. But the yard was nice and tidy, no weeds, no trash. Grass covered the bare spots. Bushes grew green and healthy on either side of the front steps. The house had been shingled, the trim painted, the porch fixed. It was hard to believe we'd ever lived there.

I stood at the gate and stared at the place so long the kids stopped playing and gathered together in a little group. Clutching cap pistols, they looked like they were protecting the family ranch from a would-be cattle rustler.

I turned away and headed back to the apartment. Too bad people couldn't fix themselves up that easily. A little paint, a little wallpaper, and you'd be ready to start over, a brand-new person.

When I walked in the door, June and Brent were too busy playing with blocks to look up and say hi. Barbara was typing. She didn't speak, either.

I tossed my jacket on the couch and went to the kitchen. Just as I was about to make myself a baloney sandwich, Barbara noticed I was home. "Please don't eat that," she called. "It's for Stu's lunch."

I slung the baloney back into the refrigerator and reached for the milk, but eagle-eyed Barbara caught me again. "Don't drink that, Gordy. We won't have enough for breakfast."

I put the milk down and slammed the refrigerator door shut. "I'm hungry," I said.

"We'll have dinner when Stu comes home from class," Barbara said. "Surely you can wait an hour."

"What are we having?" I hoped it wouldn't be Spam again. Or canned stew, another of Barbara's specialties.

"Macaroni and cheese." Clickety clack went the typewriter, faster and faster.

I glanced at the kitchen counter. Sure enough, a box of macaroni and cheese dinner sat there, along with a can of peas. That was Barbara's idea of cooking—open a box or a can, dump it in a pot, and put it on the stove. "You call this dinner?"

Barbara frowned. "What's wrong with it?"

"Grandma never made dinner from cans or boxes," I told her. "She fixed everything from scratch."

"Maybe your grandmother had more time than I do," Barbara said. "Maybe she—"

"She had twenty-four hours a day," I cut in, "just like you."

Barbara didn't have an answer for that. Grabbing a sheet of paper, she started rolling it into the typewriter. She was so mad it went in crooked. Yanking it out, she started over again. "Don't you have homework, Gordy?"

"Where am I supposed to do it? You've got stuff spread all over the table, plus there's too much noise. At Grandma's I had my own room, I had—"

"What's wrong, Gordy?" June jumped to her feet, scattering the blocks. "Why are you shouting?"

"Nothing's wrong," I yelled. "And I'm not shouting!"

"You shut up, Yuncle Poopoo," said Brent. "Or the big bad wolf will gobble you up."

Ignoring them all, I went into my so-called room, slammed the door, and flopped down on my bed. I hadn't been here a week, and nothing was going right. Opening my notebook, I began writing a letter to William. He'd sent me two letters already—keeping his promise to write even if I never answered. The second one had a kind of bitter edge to it.

"I knew you wouldn't write," he'd said. "You're having so much fun up there you've forgotten all about me."

I didn't want William to get the wrong idea, so I wrote,

For your information, I'm not having any fun at all. I hate College Hill. Barbara is a lousy cook, Stu nags me about my homework, and I have to share a room with a three-foot-high troll who snores. I'd go live in my hut down in the woods except stupid Toad and Doug burned it down by accident. They aren't so great by the way. All they ever talk about is sports and cars. They never read books, just comics. What they are, William, is D-U-M-B.

I stared at what I'd written. It was true. Compared with William, Toad and Doug *were* dumb. But they were the only friends I had. I sighed and closed my notebook. I'd finish the letter when I was in a better mood.

10

THAT NIGHT, A BIG WINTER STORM DUMPED AT LEAST twelve inches of snow on College Hill. The next day, everything shut down, including Hyattsdale High.

Around ten in the morning, Toad phoned to say he and Doug were on their way to Beech Drive with their sleds. Everybody would be there, he told me. Since I didn't have a sled, Barbara let me borrow Brent's—over his loud protests. It was pretty dinky but better than nothing.

When I got to Beech Drive, the first person I saw was Lizard, pulling a first-class Flexible Flyer and accompanied, as usual, by Magpie. You'd think those girls were Siamese twins or something. One couldn't go anywhere without the other—probably not even to the bathroom.

"Hey, G.A.S.," Lizard yelled, "what poor defenseless baby did you steal that sled from?"

I picked up a handful of snow, thinking I'd shut her

up fast. But before I had a chance to pack it hard, Lizard laughed and sped off down the hill on her sled. I belly flopped after her and knocked her into a snow-bank.

"You jerk!" Showing her great affection for me, Lizard threw a snowball at me. Hit me right in the face. For a girl, she had a good arm.

More and more kids showed up. Lizard was always in the middle of things, belly flopping down the hill, laughing louder than anyone else, shouting insults, making jokes, showing off. Every time I got a chance, I chased her and knocked her off her sled or hit her with a snowball. Even though she made it crystal clear she hated my guts, I just couldn't stay away from her.

Then Pritchett showed up. After that, I couldn't get near Lizard. He was always beside her. When he knocked her off her sled, she didn't get mad or throw snowballs at *him*. Oh, no, she just laughed. As far as Lizard was concerned, Bobby Jerk-Face Pritchett was Mister Perfect. It was enough to make me puke.

I tried to get between him and her a few times. Once the handles of his sled and mine hooked together, and Pritchett and I slid sideways down the hill, crashing into a ditch at the bottom.

"You did that on purpose, you little punk," Pritchett said, getting ugly fast.

"So?" I brushed my jacket off, hitting him in the face with a spray of snow. "Want to make something of it?"

Pritchett shoved me backward. "Stay out of my way, Smith."

"You don't own this hill," I said, shoving him back. "I'll sled where I want."

He shoved me again, a little harder. "And stay away from Elizabeth," he said. "Can't you see she doesn't want you near her?"

"Leave Lizard out of this." Now I was really mad. I shoved Pritchett so hard I slipped in the snow and fell on my face. By the time I scrambled to my feet, he'd started to walk away.

"Coward!" I hollered after him. "Why don't you run home to your mother and tell her I got snow in your face?"

Pritchett looked over his shoulder and smirked. "At least I have a mother to run home to."

His words stabbed into my heart like a knife. I had no idea anybody could cut me so deep without laying a hand on me. Busting with anger, I ran after him, calling him every cuss word I could think of.

Luckily for Pritchett, a car stopped beside him before I caught up with him. "Hop in, Bobby," I heard his father say. "You have a dental appointment this afternoon. Did you forget?"

Pritchett muttered something and slung his sled into the back seat. "See you later, Smith," he said as he rode past me.

I watched the big Buick slide around a corner and disappear. If Pritchett's old man hadn't come along, I probably would've killed him.

Well, maybe the dentist would do the deed for me. I'd heard about people dying of heart attacks when they had their teeth pulled. Pritchett was kind of young, but still—I could always hope.

Just then, Toad and Doug coasted to a stop on either side of me. "I thought you were going to beat the living daylights out of Pritchett," Doug said.

"I would have, but his father picked him up."

"Yeah, sure," Toad said. "That's why you were lying on your face in the snow."

"I slipped!"

Toad took one look at my fists and stepped back. Fortunately for him, Doug changed the subject. "See the fancy bushes in that yard?" He pointed to the house across the street. It sat right at the bottom of the hill.

I glanced at the bushes and shrugged. "They don't look like anything special to me."

"When you coast down the hill, take a shortcut across that yard and see what the guy who lives there does."

I spit in the snow, eager to hear what the guy did, but Doug was busy wiping the snot from his nose with the back of his mitten.

"This crazy professor comes out and yells if he sees you," Toad put in. "He threatens to call the cops and stuff like that."

"Cut across his yard, Gordy," Doug said. "I dare you."

I'd never been one to turn down a dare, especially when I was in the mood for trouble. Towing Brent's dinky little sled, I climbed to the top of the hill. Lizard and Magpie were still up there, tight as beads on a string. When they saw me coming, they started whispering to each other, shooting evil looks in my direction. Maybe they thought it was my fault Pritchett had left.

"Watch this, Lizard," I muttered, belly flopping downhill straight toward the professor's house. The sled's runners sang on the snow, the wind bit my face. I felt like I might take off and fly, but instead I zoomed across the professor's lawn, turning this way and that, circling bushes and laying down a great set of tracks.

Just as I swerved back to the road, I heard a door open. "Hey, you!" someone yelled. "Get off my property!"

I stopped so fast Doug plowed right into me and sent us both sprawling into the snow. To keep from crashing into us, Toad spun around and around and ended up in the professor's hedge—the kind with thorns three inches long.

The professor shook his fist and let loose a string of cuss words I couldn't have topped. "I'll call the cops if I see you boys in my yard again!" he bellowed.

We shouted a few insults at him, most of which had to do with his big belly and his wife's mustache, and then ran up Beech Drive.

When I got to the top, I spotted Lizard and Magpie in a huddle with a bunch of other girls. Just for the fun of it, I tossed a snowball at Lizard. She saw it coming and ducked. It hit a guy behind her, a tenth or eleventh grader twice my size. He and his buddies came after Toad, Doug, and me and shoved us down on our faces in the snow. They roughed us up pretty good before they lost interest in us. Of course, Lizard thought that was a scream.

Before she realized what I was doing, I tackled her and threw her down on her back. I was planning to rub snow in her face to show her just how funny it really was, but somehow I tripped and landed on top of her.

For a second, we lay there staring at each other. Lizard's face was less than an inch from mine, her cheeks rosy from the cold, her blond hair spread on the snow, her lips pink. Before I knew what I was doing, I kissed her. Right on the mouth. I didn't plan it. Didn't even think—it just happened like it was totally out of my control.

"Get off me!" Lizard thrashed around in the snow, beating me with her mittened fists. "Let me up!"

I rolled away, sort of dazed by the whole thing, and we both scrambled to our feet. I couldn't decide whether to apologize or try kissing her again.

While I was making up my mind, Lizard hauled off and slapped me so hard she made my nose bleed. It's always been sensitive, probably on account of the old man hitting it so often when I was a little kid.

I thought she might feel bad when she saw my blood spatter all over the snow, but she was too mad to notice. "How dare you?" she yelled. "How dare you kiss me?"

She wiped her mouth with the back of her mitten like she was scrubbing away my germs. "Ugh!" she spat. "I hate you, Gordy Smith! I hate, loathe, and despise you."

Grabbing her sled, Lizard ran off with Magpie. She never looked back, not once, but Magpie shot a scaredy-cat glance over her shoulder. Maybe she thought I'd chase them. Fat chance of that. Dumb girls—who needed either one of them?

Toad and Doug looked like they wanted to laugh but weren't sure they should. I picked up a handful of snow and pressed it against my nose to stop the bleeding.

"That dame needs a good punch in the old kisser," I said. What I really meant was, I wanted to kiss Lizard again—not that she'd ever let me. Without meaning to, I'd made her hate me even more than she had before. If that was possible.

Doug smacked his fist against his palm and said, "Pow! Take that, Lizard!" When I laughed, Toad figured it was safe to join in.

"Let's cut across the professor's yard again," I said, hoping they'd forget about me kissing Lizzy Lizard.

This time I got up enough speed to circle the house. I glimpsed the professor at the front door and then at the back door. By the time I slid to a stop in the middle of his lawn, he was at the front door again, hollering at me. I don't know why I did it, but instead of running, I sat on my sled and grinned at him. Scooping up a handful of snow, I bit into it. I was daring him to come after me, and he knew it.

At that moment, Doug shot past on his sled. "Throw it at him, Smith," he yelled. "I dare you."

It seemed like a good idea. I packed the snow into a ball and hurled it at the professor. Splat—it hit him in the mouth just as he was opening it wide to shout a few more curses in my direction.

I took off fast, dragging my sled over the bumps and ruts in the road. Toad and Doug were right behind me, but I wished Lizard had been there to see the expression on the professor's face when the snowball hit him. He was so surprised, his eyes almost popped out of his head. Surely she would have laughed at that.

When we'd put a few blocks between us and the professor, Toad said, "Let's go to my house. My mother's at work, so we can raid the icebox."

Toad was the only kid I knew whose parents were divorced. I'd heard his father ran away with somebody else's wife. That's why his mother had gotten a job at the factory across the train tracks. But Toad himself never talked about it. Sometimes I thought he truly believed nobody realized his dad was gone. In a town like College Hill, he should've known better.

We spent an hour or so eating just about all the food in the refrigerator and listening to the radio. Kid shows like *Jack Armstrong* and *Sky King* and *Sergeant Preston of the Yukon*—good for some laughs. Then Toad showed us a book about the facts of life his mother had given him, which was good for even more laughs.

While we looked at the book, we smoked a few of Toad's mother's cigarettes. Camels, recommended by doctors everywhere—*Your T-zone will tell you why*.

I hadn't had a smoke for so long, I almost coughed up a lung. Guess my T-zone was out of practice. If Grandma had seen me, she'd have said, "Serves you right. I hope you choke to death." Thinking of her made me feel kind of bad but not bad enough to put the dumb cigarette out.

Around five, Toad started getting nervous. "Mom should be home soon," he said, peering out the living room window.

Taking the hint, Doug and I left. It was a nice winter afternoon, not too cold, and I wasn't in a hurry to go home. After Doug headed for his house, I cut down the alley behind Lizard's house, dragging Brent's sled behind me. I was so busy staring at Lizard's kitchen windows, I didn't see Magpie till I practically bumped into her. She hadn't seen me either, probably because she was lugging a big bag of trash to the garbage can by the garage.

"What are you doing here?" she asked, as friendly as usual.

"Is this alley private property or something?"

Magpie blushed and shook her head. "I just didn't expect to see you, that's all."

She tried to step around me, but I shifted in the same direction. "Can I ask you a question?"

Magpie shrugged. The wind tugged at her hair, and she held the trash bag tighter. The look on her face reminded me of a cat cornered by a dog.

"How come you and Lizard hate me so much? Before I moved down to North Carolina, I thought we were getting along pretty good. You helped me take care of Stu, and I built you a nice tree house. Remember that?"

Magpie frowned at her feet, big as boats in a pair of

red rubber boots. "We don't hate you," she said softly. "It's just that . . ." She glanced at me, her face scarlet. "I mean, Elizabeth and me, well, we . . ."

"You what?"

Before she could answer, the back door opened and her mother stuck her head out. "Margaret, who are you talking to?"

"Nobody, Mother." With that, Magpie ducked around me, dumped the trash into the garbage can, and ran for the house.

I watched her dash up the steps two at a time, practically tripping over those big old boots. She looked back once before she disappeared inside.

"Nobody," I muttered. "She was talking to nobody."

I picked up a handful of snow, packed it tight, and threw it hard at the garbage can. *Bong*—the can tipped over and the lid flew off. Coffee grounds, empty soup cans, and chicken bones rolled across the snow.

"Nobody did that," I muttered, running down the alley toward the train tracks. "Nobody at all."

11

WHILE WE WERE EATING DINNER THAT NIGHT, THE PHONE rang. Stu picked it up. "Yes, this is Stuart Smith." There was a pause. He held the receiver tighter, his face tense. "Gordy did what?"

From where I sat, I could hear a woman's voice buzzing out of the phone like an angry wasp.

"I'm awfully sorry, Mrs. Sutcliffe," Stu said when he had a chance to speak. "Yes, certainly I'll speak to him about it."

Stu stammered a few more words of apology and hung up. I slid down in my chair and poked at the Spam on my plate. It quivered like something from outer space—where I wished I was. Stranded on an asteroid, maybe. Lost on Mars. Fighting Radar Men on the moon.

Barbara sighed. "Oh, Gordy. What now?"

"That was Toad's mother," Stu said as if I didn't

know. "She told me you were at her house this afternoon, eating her food and smoking her cigarettes. Is that true?"

"I only had one cigarette," I muttered. "I didn't even inhale."

"I don't care whether you inhaled or not," Stu said, his voice as calm and level as usual. "The point is, you have no business going into someone's house and behaving like that. Mrs. Sutcliffe was counting on the chicken for dinner. She had to give Toad tomato soup and crackers instead."

"Poor Old Mother Hubbard and her little dog Toad," I mumbled, mad my buddy had told on me. Some friend. He'd probably made it sound like it was all my fault, when he was the one who'd said we could eat whatever we wanted and smoke, too.

"Bad Yuncle Poopoo," said the troll.

Before anyone else had a chance to jump on me, the phone rang again. Stu picked up the receiver. "Professor who?" he asked.

"Oh, shoot." I braced myself for what was coming next.

When Stu hung up this time, his face was pale with anger. If he'd been Donny, he'd have hauled off and socked me, but instead he swallowed hard and said, "That was Professor Whitman."

"I was just fooling around. I didn't mean—"

But Stu was too upset to listen. "I just don't understand you, Gordy. Why do you insist on misbehaving?

Where does it get you? By now, you should have—"

"How did Whitman know who I was?" I interrupted. "He's never seen me before in his life."

Stu looked at me coldly. "If you must know, Professor Whitman got your name and phone number from Doug's parents."

Ratted on again, first by Toad and then by Doug. Next Lizard's dad would probably call and tell Stu I'd thrown his daughter down in the snow and kissed her. Everybody else had told on me. Why shouldn't Lizard join the crowd?

While I was scowling at my Spam, Barbara butted into the conversation. "I know Professor Whitman. What did Gordy do? Cut through his yard on his sled?"

To my surprise, she started to laugh. "The neighborhood kids have always done that," she went on, "just to see him come roaring outside, yelling like a madman. It's a tradition—almost a rite of passage."

I looked at Barbara hopefully. It was hard to believe, but it sounded like she might be taking up for me.

If she was, Stu was too upset to notice. "That's not all Gordy did. He damaged rare plants, cursed, and hit Whitman with a snowball."

While Stu described my behavior, June looked worried, but the troll ate it up. Eyes wide, he clutched a forkful of mashed potatoes in one hand and a soggy piece of bread in the other. I bet he couldn't wait to get big enough to do the same thing.

"Not to excuse Gordy," Barbara put in, "but Whitman

asks for it. Why, when I was little, I—" She covered her mouth to keep from laughing again.

"What did you do to him?" I asked, eager to keep Barbara talking. If she got started on a funny story, Stu might relax and see the whole thing as the joke I'd meant it to be. The kind of thing Henry Aldrich might do. People in the radio audience howled with laughter when he pulled silly stunts. If Henry could get away with it, why couldn't I?

But Barbara let me down. "Oh, it was nothing, nothing at all," she said. Turning back into a grown-up, she frowned at Brent. "Please don't play with your food, honey. Either eat your bread or put it down."

Brent made a fist and slowly squeezed the bread till it oozed out between his fingers. The expression on his face was like seeing myself in a mirror—sometimes it was hard to believe the troll and I weren't blood kin after all.

"Pop made all of us miserable," Stu said, ignoring the mess the troll was making, "but you can't go on rebelling against authority all your life, Gordy. You need to change your attitude. You should try to . . ."

While Stu droned on, I fidgeted with a crust of bread and let his words wash over me like rain. He was taking a psychology course, and most of what he said sounded like it came right out of a book.

Stu leaned toward me to get my attention. "I know it was different at Grandma's," he said. "You had your own room, you—"

I slid lower in my chair, more determined than ever not to listen. What did Stu know about Grandma's house that I didn't already know?

Finally he ran out of words—or just gave up. "Don't you have anything to say for yourself?" he asked me.

"I'm sorry," I muttered, meaning I was sorry Toad and Doug told on me, sorry the professor and Mrs. Sutcliffe called Stu, sorry Stu was sore at me—but not especially sorry for my so-called crimes. After all, I hadn't done anything *that* bad. The professor was a nut. Barbara had even said so.

Stu sat back in his chair. The troll happily poured milk into a hole he'd made in his mashed potatoes. June sniffed and wiped her nose with the back of her hand. Barbara patted Stu's hand and turned to me. "What do you think we should do about this, Gordy?"

Several possibilities floated through my head—draw and quarter Toad and Doug for telling on me, torch Whitman's rare plants, blow up his house, run away. For obvious reasons, I kept these thoughts to myself. They weren't the sort of answers Barbara wanted.

"How about writing them each a letter of apology?" she asked.

Stu stared at her. "Do you think that's sufficient?"

She shrugged. "It's what my parents always made me do."

It sounded good to me, but Stu looked doubtful. Which wasn't surprising. After all, what did he know about such things? Compared with the old man's methods, writing a letter was nothing.

Stu sighed. "Okay, Gordy, write the letters, but don't think you can get away with scribbling a few words on a piece of paper. Spell correctly. Punctuate. Maybe you can learn something in the process."

I fussed and moaned and groaned, but deep down inside I felt like Brer Rabbit begging Brer B'ar not to throw him in the briar patch. Thanks to Grandma, I'd had plenty of practice writing apologies.

"Just get on with it, Gordy," Stu said wearily. "I've got a paper to write and a botany exam to study for. I don't have time to argue with you."

After I'd written my apologies to Mrs. Sutcliffe and the professor, I decided to finish my letter to William. He'd now sent me four, none of which I'd answered. In the last one he'd said, "Don't write. See if I care. Some people have moved into your grandmother's house and I'm friends with one of them."

I didn't like to think of strangers making changes in Grandma's house, painting the walls, getting new furniture, hanging pictures. Someone in my old room. Someone in Grandma's room.

Most of all, I hated the idea of William being friends with one of them.

Picking up where I'd left off last time, I wrote,

Today I got in trouble three times. I threw a snowball at this crazy professor and I had to write him an apology letter. I also ate the food Toad's mother was saving for dinner, so I had to write her a letter, too. The best thing was, I kissed this snobby girl, Lizard. She got mad, but at least she didn't tell on me, so I didn't have to write her a letter.

While I thought about what I'd say next, I doodled a few fighter planes at the bottom of my notebook paper. A German Heinkel was going down in flames. I liked the look of pure fear I'd drawn on the pilot's face.

I wanted to tell William how much I missed having him to talk to. How lonesome I was. How blue I felt. How much I missed him and Grandma. But only chumps admitted that kind of stuff. And I was no chump. So this is what I wrote:

I knew you'd make a new friend as soon as I left. I bet your mother likes him better than me and lets him sleep over every Saturday night. She probably even bought a television set for you and him to watch.

When I signed off, I copied what William had written at the end of all his letters: "As ever, Gordy."

Nothing sappy about that. Besides, it was true. Gordy Smith was just as bad as ever. William could ask anybody in College Hill, including Stu. They'd tell him.

12

SCHOOL STAYED CLOSED FOR TWO DAYS. TO KEEP ME OUT of trouble, Barbara came up with the great idea of putting me in charge of June and the troll. That meant taking them on sled rides and building snowmen, which the troll always knocked down. He just loved wrecking stuff.

Inside, we played Uncle Wiggly, Chutes and Ladders, Winnie the Pooh, and other dumb board games. If Brent lost, he threw tantrums. I had to figure out ways to cheat so he'd win. Of course, June caught me and complained. It wasn't fair, she said, and she upset the board, scattering the playing pieces. It took me ages to find them all.

Believe me, I was glad the day school reopened. Anything was better than another game of Uncle Wiggly.

I met Toad and Doug at the streetcar stop. It was the first time I'd seen them since our little picnic at Toad's house. They looked kind of nervous—as well they might, the dirty tale-telling rats.

"Hey, Gordo, you're not sore, are you?" Doug asked, his voice going up a few notes. "I told my father not to give your phone number to Whitman. But he just went ahead and did it anyway. It wasn't my fault, honest."

Toad edged a little closer to Doug. "I never told Mom you were at our house, Gordy. She guessed. That's how she is. I swear she can read my mind or something, I can't keep anything from her. She—"

I don't know how long Toad would have babbled about his mother if I hadn't told him to shut up. "Just keep your lip buttoned next time, okay?" I spat into an icy puddle at Toad's feet. "I don't think much of stool pigeons."

It was the first time I'd felt in charge since I'd come back to College Hill.

At lunch, I saw Lizard on the other side of the cafeteria. She was wearing a fuzzy pink sweater that fit even better than the blue one. As usual, Pritchett was hanging all over her.

Toad poked my side. "You just can't keep your eyes off her, can you?"

"Who?" I asked.

Doug snickered. "Admit it, Smith. You're in love with Lizard Crawford. Don't forget, we were there when you kissed her."

Toad puckered his lips and made loud smooching noises. "Oh, baby, baby," he moaned.

I scowled at my sandwich, another of Barbara's peanut butter and jelly specials. The baloney and cheese were reserved for Stu—which seemed unfair, since I was still growing and probably needed more nourishment than he did. But that's life—U-N-F-A-I-R.

"I bet Pritchett's taking her to the Sweetheart Dance," Doug said.

I looked up from my sandwich. "The Sweetheart Dance? What's that?"

Toad belched in disbelief and Doug shook his head. "Haven't you seen the posters? The whole school's plastered with them."

"Maybe you should ask Lizard to go with you." Doug started laughing like it was a big joke or something. "Just in case Pritchett hasn't gotten around to it yet."

Toad joined in the guffaws, but I smashed my milk carton flat and scowled at both of them. "Maybe I should," I muttered, which made my so-called buddies laugh even louder.

"I dare you," Toad said.

"I double dare you!" Doug added, still laughing.

"I wouldn't be seen dead at a dance," I said, sneering at the idea of me, Gordy Smith, sashaying around the gym with a girl.

But that afternoon in math I found myself thinking how nice it would be to dance with Lizard. I'd put my arms around her, hold her close, maybe even sing in her ear. Too bad the only songs I knew were "The Woody Woodpecker Song," "Open the Door, Richard," and "The

Too-Fat Polka." It was hard to imagine getting romantic with a line like "I don't want her, you can have her, she's too fat for me."

Well, I had a week. That was more than enough time to learn a few corny love songs.

After school, I gave Toad and Doug the slip and went looking for Lizard. It was one of those days you sometimes get in February. The wind had turned warm and soft, and all that was left of the snow were little gray piles, pockmarked with cinders from the trains.

For once I was lucky. At the playground, I spotted Lizard pushing Brent in a swing while Magpie and June climbed on the jungle gym. June smiled and waved, but no one else even glanced my way. I didn't let that stop me. Grabbing a swing next to Brent, I was soon pumping higher than Lizard could push him.

The troll didn't like that. "Higher, Lizbeth, higher!" he shouted. "Like Yuncle Poopoo!"

Lizard did her best, jumping to push the swing, but she couldn't catch me.

Hoping to impress her, I took a flying leap when the swing was at its highest and landed neatly on my feet, a trick Bobby Pritchett couldn't have done if he'd tried. But Lizard didn't even look.

Brent tried to jump the way I had. But he tumbled into the mud and started howling. Naturally Lizard blamed it on me. "How am I going to explain the mud all over his jacket? Barbara will think it's my fault!"

Giving me a nasty look, Lizard stalked over to one of the seesaws. She put Brent on one end and balanced herself on the other. Going up and down soothed the troll, and he finally stopped bawling.

I stood there for a while, trying to come up with something to say—"Nice day, huh? Think we'll get any more snow? Read any good books lately?" Finally I gave up and sat down behind Brent on the seesaw, trapping Lizard in the air. Now she had to listen to me.

She scowled down at me. "Gordy Smith, if you jump off and bump me, I'll kill you!"

"That's kid stuff," I said, wishing she'd give me credit for growing up some since sixth grade.

"Get off, Yuncle Poopoo, get off." The troll pushed at me. "Let Lizbeth seesaw me!"

I stared over the troll's head at Lizard. My heart was pounding so fast I could hardly breathe, but I figured it was now or never. The worst she could say was no. That wouldn't kill me. Much.

"How'dyouliketogototheSweetheartDancewithme?" I asked, speaking so fast my invitation came out in a big clump.

"What?" Lizard stared at me as if I'd insulted her with a string of dirty words.

"The Sweetheart Dance," I yelled. "Would you like to go with me?"

"Go with *you*? Are you crazy? I wouldn't be seen dead with you!"

"Why the hell not?" I was so mad I slipped up and cussed—which I hadn't meant to do.

"For one thing I *hate* you, and for another I already have a date!"

"With that jerk Bobby Pritchett?"

Lizard's face got even redder. "Bobby's not a jerk!"

"I could beat him to a pulp."

"Fighting—is that the only thing you know how to do?"

The scorn in Lizard's voice cut me to the heart. Without looking at her, I got off the seesaw. I hoped her end would hit the ground hard, but Brent slowed it down.

I didn't look back until I was halfway across the playground. Lizard was standing beside the seesaw, hands on her hips, glaring at me. Brent stood beside her, sticking out his tongue.

"I was only kidding about the dance," I yelled at her. "I wouldn't be seen dead with you either!"

I forced myself to walk away slowly, swinging my arms and whistling "The Too-Fat Polka." Lizard Crawford had just busted my heart, but she'd never know it.

13

THE NEXT DAY I DREADED GOING TO SCHOOL. SUPPOSE Lizard had spread it all over College Hill that I'd invited her to the Sweetheart Dance? Tough guy Smith asked a girl for a date and got turned down. Har de har har har.

I tried faking the bellyache of all bellyaches, but it didn't fool Barbara. She just patted me on the head and said, "Do you have a test today, Gordy?"

When she threatened to give me her special treatment—castor oil in orange juice—I dragged myself out of the apartment. Anything was better than that nasty stuff.

Toad and Doug met me at the streetcar stop. To my relief, they acted normal, so I figured they hadn't heard anything. Yet.

At Garfield Road, Magpie and Lizard got on and took a seat near the front. They didn't look at me, but I knew they knew exactly where I was sitting.

"Now's your chance, Gordy." Toad gave me a shove that almost made me fall off my seat. "Ask her."

"Quick," Doug said, giving me an even harder push. "Before Pritchett gets on."

"Lay off," I yelled, pushing Doug back.

Suddenly all three of us landed on the floor, scattering books and papers everywhere.

The streetcar slowed for Cherry Road, and the driver glanced over his shoulder. "Okay, you three, off. If I've told you once, I've told you a dozen times. No horseplay on my car."

"But we already paid," I said.

"And we'll be late for school," Toad wailed.

"Tough," said the driver. "Remember that the next time you feel like cutting up."

There was a crowd of kids waiting to get on, so Toad and Doug and I had to push our way through them. I managed to bump Pritchett so he stumbled getting on and almost knocked a girl down. I was hoping he'd get kicked off, too, but the driver just said, "Quit fooling around and sit down."

As the streetcar pulled away, I saw Lizard make a face at me. I gave her the finger, but I don't think she noticed.

It was a half hour's walk to school. Even if we ran, we wouldn't get there before the bell, so we slouched along, taking our time. As Grandma used to say, "Better to be hanged as a sheep than a goat," or something like that. I never was too sure what it meant. But I knew one thing for sure. Grandma would have been furious if she'd seen me get kicked off that streetcar.

"You can always ask Lizard at lunch," Toad said. "Or on the way home."

I kicked a stone hard and watched it sail through the air. "For your information, stupid, I asked her yesterday, and she said no."

Toad shrugged. "It figures."

"Good thing I didn't bet on her saying yes," Doug said.

By the time we got to school it was ten past nine, and we had to see Mueller. "Twenty minutes of detention," he said, handing us each a scribbled note for our homeroom teachers. "Next time it will be an hour."

After we got out of detention, Toad, Doug, and I fooled around at the Trolley Stoppe Shoppe, playing pinball and listening to the jukebox. We sang "Open the Door, Richard" so loud we got kicked out for being rowdy.

Toad and Doug went home, but I didn't feel like going back to the apartment. What was the point? The troll would be running around screeching, June would be listening to *Sky King*, Stu would be trying to study, and Barbara would either be typing or whipping up some great concoction for dinner. We hadn't had Spam all week, so more than likely that's what I'd smell when I walked in the door.

I walked up to Route 1, thinking I might stop at the Little Tavern for one of their lousy hamburgers—deathballs, we called them. Eating one of those might make the Spam go down easier.

Before I got to the Little Tavern, though, I saw Lizard and Magpie go into the record store across the highway. If I'd had any sense, I would have bought my hamburger and gone home. I'd avoided Lizard all day at school. Why was I running across Route 1, dodging cars and trucks, to follow her now? It didn't make any sense, but I just couldn't stay away from that little snot.

I found the two of them in the back of the store, flipping through albums. Neither one saw me. They were too busy looking at the records.

"Here it is, Margaret!" Lizard pulled an album out of the bin and waved it in Magpie's face.

I sidled closer to see the cover—*Carousel*, one of those sappy Broadway musicals. A three-record set. Lizard had expensive taste.

Hugging the album, Lizard closed her eyes and spun around humming "If I Loved You" while Magpie giggled. By sheer luck, Lizard whirled right into me. If I'd known how, I'd have waltzed her around the record shop, up one aisle and down the other, but instead I just held her, enjoying being close enough to smell her hair.

My bliss didn't last long. Pulling away from me, Lizard turned scarlet. "Get your hands off me, Gordy Smith! Can't I go anywhere without seeing your ugly face?"

I let my eyes stray to the album, mainly because it was covering Lizard's chest. "So is that your favorite record or something?"

"None of your beeswax!" She turned away, clutching the album tighter.

It was Lizard's big mouth that got the clerk's attention, not mine. In a flash he was beside us, a tall, skinny college guy with a huge Adam's apple and a bad case of acne—not what I'd call the intimidating type.

"Are you planning to buy something today?" he asked, looking straight at me—big bad Gordy Smith.

I snatched *Carousel* out of Lizard's hand. I had one dollar in my pocket—my streetcar, lunch, and milk money for the week. But I'd have gladly given it to Lizard. Waving the album at the clerk, I asked, "How much is this?"

He snatched it out of my hand. "More than you can afford, twerp!"

I watched him put *Carousel* back in the rack with the other albums. "You ought to give up chocolate," I said. "You might get rid of those zits."

The guy glared at me. "That's enough. Get out of here and don't come back till you learn some manners."

"That'll be never! " Lizard glared at me like she wanted to cut my heart out and eat it for dinner.

Giving the clerk one of my best smirks, I took Lizard and Magpie by the arm like a guy in a movie—Humphrey Bogart maybe. Or James Cagney. "Let's blow this joint, ladies."

The two of them stared at me like I was something out of their worst nightmare. Yanking their arms free, they flounced out of the store ahead of me. I guessed they didn't watch the same movies I did.

On the sidewalk, Lizard faced me. "Do you have to

ruin everything, Gordy Smith? That guy used to let us sit in a booth and listen to records all day. Now, thanks to you, he'll never let us through the front door again!"

I pulled my wrinkled dollar bill out of my pocket. "I was going to loan you this," I said. "You could've bought the dumb album and told that SOB to kiss your royal behind."

"A dollar—if you think you can buy that album for a dollar you're even dumber than I thought!" Lizard yelled. "You and your money and your dirty mouth can just get lost!"

Magpie didn't say a word. From the expression on her face, I guessed she was shocked speechless. Without looking back, the two of them ran across Route 1 and headed toward Calvert Road. I watched them till they were out of sight.

Talk about bad manners—Lizard hadn't even thanked me for offering to help her buy that crummy album. I bet Bobby Jerk-Face Pritchett wouldn't have given her *his* last dollar.

No longer in the mood for a deathball, I walked home, feeling even crummier than usual. Every time I tried to please Lizard, something went wrong and she ended up hating me more than before. If she'd just give me a chance, she'd see I was a lot nicer than I used to be. Not perfect, of course. But who is?

14

I'D BEEN RIGHT ABOUT DINNER. BARBARA HAD TRIED TO dress up the main dish with canned pineapple slices, but nothing could disguise the nasty taste or slimy feel of Spam.

After we ate, I sat at the table trying to do my math problems. At my feet, the troll was playing with his toy cars and trucks, crashing them into one another and making siren sounds. June was listening to Henry Aldrich on the radio and laughing along with the audience. In the kitchen, Barbara was telling Stu about the new houses going up on Rhode Island Avenue.

"They'll be selling for less than ten thousand," she said. "When you get the money from your grandmother's estate, we could use it as a down payment."

There was a little silence. Then Stu said, "Don't get your hopes up, Barb."

"Between your salary, my typing, and what we get

for June and Gordy, I'm positive we can manage, Stu." She hesitated a moment. "I could write to Mother and Daddy. When they come up for their next visit, maybe they—"

"I've told you how I feel about that," Stu said. "I want us to make it on our own. When I graduate and get a job teaching—"

"We can't go on living in this apartment, Stu." Barbara turned on the water and began washing the dinner dishes. "There's no room for anything!" She punctuated every word with a splash or a clink. It sounded like she might break all the glasses just to make her point.

When Stu didn't answer, she asked if he'd at least look at the houses. "I've already picked my favorite model," she said, "a nice little brick bungalow with dormers. It would be just right for us. Three bedrooms upstairs and a basement rec room where Gordy could sleep."

I held my breath and crossed my fingers and hoped with all my heart. My own bedroom down in the basement, far from the troll, a place where I could have some privacy, a place to think my thoughts and read and write letters to William. "Say yes, Stu, say yes," I whispered. "Yes, yes, yes."

"I guess we could take a look next week after I get off work." Stu put his arms around Barbara and gave her a hug, but he sounded as worried as ever.

I tried one more math problem. Brent crashed a truck into my foot. June shrieked, "Henry, Henry Aldrich" along with the radio. Barbara dropped a pot or something. Slamming my book shut, I grabbed my jacket and went out.

Before I got to the bottom of the steps, Stu came after me. "Hold it, Gordy!" he shouted.

On the second floor, a door flew open and Mrs. Reilly stuck her head out. "Will you be quiet?" she hollered at Stu. "I just got my baby to sleep!" Behind her a kid started wailing.

"Sorry," Stu said, slinking past like a dog with its tail between its legs.

Mrs. Reilly slammed her door, but we could still hear the baby crying. She'd probably waked it herself yelling at us.

Stu followed me outside. "Where are you going, Gordy?"

"I can't stand being cooped up in there another minute," I said, taking a deep breath of fresh air. "Barbara's right. You ought to buy a house. Not just because of June and me, but to get away from old bags like Mrs. Reilly."

Stu stood on the sagging porch steps and stared glumly into the dark. Not far away, a train whistle blew. The Calvert Road crossing signal flashed red and the bell started ringing. A few seconds later, I saw the locomotive's light. The whistle blew again, and the freight rumbled past, shaking the porch.

When the train was gone, the night seemed very quiet. Down in the swamp across the tracks, tree toads peeped, a sign spring was coming.

"It's not easy for Barb to live here," Stu said. "She's used to nicer things."

I nodded, remembering Barbara's parents' house and how big it was. Probably Mr. and Mrs. Fisher had an even better place in Florida, with palm trees and stuff. Flamingos and alligators, too.

"If you'd stayed in the army," I muttered, "you could have gotten a GI loan and bought a house with that. It would have paid for college, too."

Stu looked at me. "You know how I feel about the military. Why bring it up?"

"Maybe because people are always saying stuff about it."

Stu put his arm around my shoulders. "I'm sorry it bothers you, Gordy."

I pulled away. "You shouldn't apologize all the time. It makes you sound like a chump."

Stu shrugged and opened the door. "Come back inside, Gordy. I'll help you with your math."

"No, thanks," I said. "It's a nice night. I think I'll take a walk."

Stu hesitated like he didn't think it was a good idea to turn me loose. "Be back by eight," he said.

"Come on, Stu, it's already past seven. Let me stay out at least till nine."

Before he could answer, Barbara came downstairs. "Stu, Brent wants you to read him a story."

Stu sighed and turned to me. "Eight-thirty, Gordy. And not a minute later."

I headed down Erskine, thinking I might see what

Toad was up to, but when I got to Garfield, I decided to walk past Lizard's house. A light was on in the living room, and I could see the blue glow of her television set. I stood at the end of her sidewalk for a few minutes, wishing I had the nerve to walk up her steps and ring the bell. She'd open the door and invite me in. We'd sit on the couch, eat popcorn, and watch television. Maybe Lizard would let me kiss her, a real kiss this time—no slap afterward, no bloody nose. Fat chance of that.

I walked on, wishing I could do something to make Lizard like me. What if I bought her a present? A box of candy, maybe. Flowers. Or better yet, what if I gave her that album she loved so much? Maybe she'd be so grateful she'd break her date with Pritchett and go to the dance with me—Gordon P. Smith, Esquire.

The trouble was that Lizard had been right about my dollar. It wouldn't buy a three record boxed set like *Carousel.* I don't know why I'd even offered it to her.

But suppose I stole the album? If I got away with it, Lizard would never sneer at me again. How could she? She'd be so happy to have *Carousel,* she'd forgive me for every stupid thing I'd done to her in elementary school. She'd be my girlfriend. It would be my jokes she laughed at, my hand she held walking home from the streetcar. For a payoff like that, no risk was too great.

Before I went inside, I looked through the record shop window. A different guy sat at the cash register, talking to a bunch of giggly college girls. Without giving him a glance, I strolled to the back of the store and started thumbing through the albums till I found *Carousel.*

Trying to act casual, I read the back of the box. It was the story of a guy who worked for a carnival. He treated this girl real bad, but after he died he was given a chance to come to back to earth for one day to prove he wasn't a worthless bum after all. Just the kind of corny stuff dames went nuts over.

In the front of the store, I heard one of the college girls say, "I can't believe you don't like Frank Sinatra! We just adore him."

"I prefer big bands," the guy said. "I've got almost every record Glenn Miller ever made. Tommy Dorsey, Benny Goodman, Duke Ellington."

"Oh, I love swing," the girl said quickly. "How about Woody Herman? Isn't he fabulous?"

While the girls swooned all over the clerk, I slid *Carousel* under my jacket and walked out of the store, taking my time, trying to act natural, hoping nobody but me could hear my heart thumping.

Once I was safely on the other side of Route 1, I ran into the dark, empty lot behind the Little Tavern and collapsed against a fence, sure I'd never breathe normally again. It was the first time I'd stolen anything bigger than a pack of gum or a candy bar, and I was scared sick. Not that I'd have admitted it—if Doug and Toad had been with me, I would've tricked them into thinking I was a natural-born thief, afraid of nothing.

But the way I felt now, I was glad I didn't have to make the effort.

As soon as my legs steadied, I headed for Lizard's house, but, when I got there, I didn't have the nerve to ring her doorbell—probably because her father's police car was parked in front. While I hesitated, a light went on upstairs. A couple of seconds later, I saw Lizard pass the window. Her bedroom—she was in her bedroom.

If only she had a balcony. I'd climb up like Romeo and make a flowery speech, maybe even kiss her. But there wasn't a vine, bush, or tree anywhere near the house. I'd have to try something else.

Crouching down, I crept into Lizard's yard like a spy sneaking through enemy territory, staying in the shadows, making no noise. When I was under her window, I hurled a couple of pebbles at it. They clicked and clacked against the glass, but nothing happened.

I threw a few more. Finally Lizard came to the window and peered down at me. I could tell I was the last person she'd expected to see. Or wanted to see, for that matter. But she raised the sash and leaned out. "Gordy Smith," she hissed, "get out of my yard. Right now. Or I'll call my dad."

"Wait," I whispered. "Don't get mad. Don't call your old man, either. Let me tell you something first."

"What makes you think I want to hear anything you have to say?"

"I came to apologize," I said quickly, scared she'd slam the window shut and pull the blind down, too. "I'm sorry I goofed off in the record store, I'm sorry I bumped you on the seesaw yesterday, I'm sorry I asked you to the dumb dance, I'm sorry I got fresh with you in the snow. In fact, I'm sorry for everything I ever did to you—all the way back to kindergarten."

There. Now let her say I had bad manners. Grandma herself couldn't have gotten a more polite apology out of me. And it had been my own idea. Nobody had made me do it.

Lizard stared at me. "You're apologizing? You? Gordy Smith? Pinch me, I must be dreaming."

I held the album up. "Look. I have a present for you. A peace offering."

"What is it?" Lizard leaned farther out the window. "I can't tell from here."

"Come down and see. I'll wait for you in the alley." When she hesitated, I added, "It's something really nice, honest it is."

"This better not be a trick." Giving me a long, hard look, Lizard lowered her window. I didn't know whether she'd come or not, she hadn't said, but I ran across her backyard and ducked into the garage's shadow. I hoped she wouldn't send her big brother, Joe—or worse yet, her father.

The cocker spaniels across the alley started running up and down their side of the fence, barking and growling at me. Just as I was thinking I'd better run before somebody saw me, a woman yelled, "Bad dogs! Be quiet! How many times have I told you to ignore that stupid cat?"

At the same moment, Lizard stepped around the

corner of the garage. Her hair was silver in the moonlight, her face pale. She was wearing her fuzzy pink sweater and a pair of blue jeans. No jacket—I guessed she wasn't planning to stay long.

"I must be crazy," she said. "My dad would kill me if he knew I was out here talking to you. I don't even know why I came."

I didn't know what to say, what to do. I'd never been alone in the dark with a girl before. So I stood there like a dummy, holding the album behind my back, hoping she'd try to grab it.

But Lizard kept her distance. "I thought you said you had something for me."

"I do."

She tossed her head, and her hair swirled around her face like cotton candy. "What makes you think I want it, G.A.S.?"

I swallowed down my annoyance at being called G.A.S. "Trust me for once," I muttered.

"Don't make me laugh." Lizard began edging away. "I wouldn't trust you to take out the trash."

As usual, things weren't working out the way I'd hoped. Scared she'd leave, I thrust the album at her. "Here. Now you don't have to go to the record shop. You can hear it whenever you want."

Lizard took the album and stared at the cover. "Where did you get the money to buy this? I've been saving my baby-sitting money for ages."

I shoved my hands deeper into my pockets and shrugged, not sure how to answer Lizard's question.

Should I tell her I bought it? Or would she be more impressed if I told her the truth? Anybody could buy a record album, Pritchett included. But how many guys loved Lizard enough to swipe one for her?

Lizard studied my face. "You didn't steal it, did you?"

Misreading the look in her eyes, I grinned. "The guy at the record shop was so dumb I could have walked out with a dozen albums under my jacket and he wouldn't have noticed. But all I took was *Carousel*—for you, Lizard, so you—"

"You stole this?" Lizard stepped back and stared at me, her eyes wide. Before I knew what she was doing, she threw the album at me. "Do you think I want something you *stole*?"

"But, Lizard, I—"

"You're going to end up in jail, Gordy Smith! And the sooner the better!" With that, she turned and ran into her yard.

"Wait, Lizard." Leaving the album in the dirt, I dashed after her and caught her arm to stop her from going inside. "I just thought—"

Lizard jerked away and swung at me. I ducked before she could start another nosebleed.

"You don't understand!" Grabbing her sleeve, I pulled her toward me. I wanted to tell her I loved her, but the words stuck in my throat. So I tried to kiss her instead.

At that moment the back porch light came on and lit the whole yard. The door flew open, and Mr. Crawford stepped outside. "Get in the house, Elizabeth!" he yelled. "And you, Smith, beat it!"

For all I knew, Crawford had a gun pointed at me. Stopping just long enough to pick up the album, I headed for the train tracks as fast as my feet would take me. A locomotive was coming, blotting out the stars with smoke. I opened the album and hurled the records through the air like flying saucers. They hit the tracks, and the train ground them to bits, scattering the songs like cinders.

I tossed the empty album into the weeds and walked off. The moon floated along beside me, its face glum. If the so-called man in the moon could have talked, he'd have said, "Boy, are you dumb, Gordy Smith. Now she *really* hates you."

15

THE NEXT DAY AT LUNCH, TOAD TOLD DOUG AND ME HE'D heard you could go to the Sweetheart Dance without a date. It was called going stag, he said.

At first I said it was a stupid idea, but by Friday I'd changed my mind. Although I'd probably be sorry, I wanted to see Lizard. Maybe I'd do something to impress her, something to make her like me better than Pritchett. What it would be I didn't know. The record hadn't worked. Maybe nothing would.

I borrowed Stu's one and only sports coat and walked to Doug's house. Mr. Murray drove the three of us to school. When we were almost there, he said, "Are you sure you boys don't want me to come back when the dance is over and take you home?"

"I told you we're going to the Hot Shoppe afterward," Doug said. "That's what everybody does—you know, to get french fries and hamburgers and shakes."

Mr. Murray sighed and let us out of the car a block

away from the school. Doug's idea—he didn't want anyone to see us getting out of his father's car, an old Ford with a busted headlight.

"Be home by eleven," Mr. Murray said, "and for God's sake, behave yourself."

Doug saluted. "Yes, sir."

I touched my clip-on bow tie to make sure it was still attached to my shirt collar and smoothed my hair. Barbara had combed it back with some of Stu's Vitalis, and it felt as stiff as if she'd shellacked it. Even worse than my hair was Stu's sports coat. It was so big, I looked like the movie star Charlie Chaplin. The little tramp, they called him.

"Come on," Toad muttered. "Let's see what's what."

We sauntered through the gym doors like we went to dances every Friday night, which was a laugh since none of us knew the first thing about it. We'd just had three weeks of social dancing in phys. ed., supposedly learning the two-step and the jitterbug, but I'd spent most of the time hiding. I hated the girls in my class. They must have been the snobbiest bunch in the whole school. You'd think I had both bad breath and BO, the way they acted. Plus every one of them was taller than me. A class of giantesses, that's what they were.

The gym was decorated with red and white crepe paper streamers, and the walls were plastered with hearts cut from red construction paper, but the place still smelled like sweat and old tennis shoes. The lights were dimmed, though, and the phys. ed. teachers had set up a table for the record player. They sat behind it, picking records and keeping an eye on us. No smiles, no laughs—they were the wardens and we were the inmates. One sign of trouble, and they'd call in the riot squad.

The first girl I saw was Magpie. She was sitting on a folding chair with a bunch of other girls, all pretending they'd come to the gym to talk to one another, not to dance. Except for her glasses and being so tall and skinny, Magpie looked pretty good in a blue dress made out of some kind of silky stuff. Her hair was curled, and she'd put on a little bit of pale pink lipstick. Nylon stockings, too, and flat-soled shiny black shoes that must have been size thirteen.

Lizard was out on the gym floor jitterbugging with Pritchett. She was wearing a blue dress, too. The top was made of something soft, velvet I guess, and the skirt was full and rustly. Her hair reminded me of the gold Rumpelstiltskin spun in that old fairy tale.

Just looking at her made me want to punch Pritchett. Especially when the record changed to a dumb love song and he started slow dancing with her, holding her close, pressing his cheek against her cheek.

"Why don't you cut in on her?" Toad asked me. "See if she'll dance with you?"

"Bad idea, Toad. She'll slap Gordy and make his nose bleed again." Doug glanced at me, smirking a little. "I bet you wouldn't have the nerve anyway."

I glared at Doug. "What's the use? I can't dance."

Toad studied the couples gliding around the gym in slow motion. "It doesn't look so hard," he said. "You just hold her tight and kind of shuffle and sway to the music."

"Nobody expects you to be Fred Astaire," Doug said.

Toad snorted. "Gordy's chicken. He's scared of Bobby."

Lizard danced past, smiling at Pritchett. For a second our eyes met. Then, with perfect timing, Doug gave me a shove and I bumped into Lizard and Pritchett. They stopped and glared at me, but I figured I might as well take advantage of the situation. "May I cut in?" I asked Lizard.

Lizard looked like she couldn't believe I'd dared insult her again. But before she could say anything, Pritchett said, "No, you can't, shorty."

I shoved my jaw at him. "Says who?"

"Says *me*." Lizard put her hand on Pritchett's shoulder and gave him a smile so sweet it almost made me puke. "Shall we dance, Bobby?"

"Let's get some punch, Gordy," Toad said. If he hadn't stepped between me and Pritchett, the jerk would have gotten some punch, too—the pow-in-the-kisser kind.

On the way to the refreshment table, I ran into Magpie—bumped right into her and made her spill her drink. Luckily, it missed her dress and hit the floor with a splash. Her face turned crimson like she was scared people would think she'd wet her pants or something.

"Sorry, Magpie," I muttered.

"It's okay," she whispered, edging away from me. It was the first time I'd been near her since we'd gotten thrown out of the record store, so I guessed she was still sore about that. Or maybe she was scared to turn her back on me. As far as I could figure, Magpie thought I was the devil himself come to College Hill just to torment her.

So I was surprised when Magpie continued our conversation. "I didn't think you'd be here," she said, which I translated as meaning she'd hoped I wouldn't show my ugly face.

"It was Toad and Doug's idea. Not mine. I'll probably leave soon." I looked around for my buddies, but they'd disappeared into the crowd around the refreshment table. Knowing Toad, they'd stay there till every crumb was gone.

Magpie cleared her throat. "I'm stuck here till Elizabeth leaves. I came with her and Bobby. Jeff came, too, but I don't know where he went." She looked around uneasily. "It wasn't exactly a date. Just a ride, I guess."

I didn't know what to say. It sounded like Jeff had dumped poor old Magpie.

"I think he came with me so he could see Sonia Higgins," Magpie went on. "That's who he really likes, but she likes Tony Reynolds."

"Sonia's a snot," I said, "and Jeff's a jerk."

Magpie twisted her paper napkin around one finger and cleared her throat again. "Do you know how to dance, Gordy?"

I shook my head, scared she wanted me to dance with her. I only came up to her chin, for Pete's sake. We would have looked ridiculous.

"I'm not very good at it," Magpie admitted.

"Then how come you're here?"

She blushed and shrugged her skinny shoulders. "I was on the decorating committee," she said. "I wanted to see how the gym would look with the lights and all. It's beautiful, isn't it?"

I shrugged and tried to think of something to say that wouldn't hurt her feelings. "It's okay, I guess."

Out on the gym floor, Lizard and Pritchett were jitterbugging to "Pennsylvania 6-5000," an old Glenn Miller song I remembered hearing way back during the war. Every time Pritchett twirled Lizard, her skirt spun out, showing a lot of good-looking leg. One consolation—I was probably getting a better view than he was.

Magpie must have noticed who I was looking at because she said, "I wish I was as good a dancer as Elizabeth."

"She's not so hot," I lied.

Just then the music stopped, and Lizard and Pritchett walked over to us. Neither seemed pleased to see me—which wasn't surprising.

"Margaret, I've been looking all over for you." Lizard grabbed Magpie's arm and pulled her away from me like I was dangerous. Darting a dirty look at me, Lizard whispered something in Magpie's ear that made them both giggle.

While the girls traded jokes, Pritchett looked me up and down, his eyes narrow. "Fine-looking jacket, Smith."

"Glad you like it," I said, matching his sarcasm.

"Maybe in two or three years you'll grow into it."

I tried to think of a snappy comeback, but nothing came to mind—probably because Lizard was staring at me like I'd just crawled out from under a rock. A runt, a midget, a dwarf, that's all I was to her.

Pritchett sneered down at me. "Tell me something, Smith. Is your father still in jail?"

"No, you jerk. He's in California." In my pockets, my hands tightened into fists. Pritchett was definitely asking for it.

"Oh, so you admit he *used* to be in jail—him and the deserter both." Pritchett smirked at Lizard. "Great family, huh? Jailbirds, drunks, unpatriotic cowards."

Lizard drew in her breath, but I didn't give her a chance to add any insults. Stepping closer to Pritchett, I showed him my fists. "You better shut your mouth, you SOB. before I shut it for you."

Pritchett grinned. "Don't make me laugh, shorty. I bet you're just as yellow as your brother."

That was all I was going to take. I drew back my fist and punched Pritchett as hard as I could, knocking him flat.

He was on his feet in a second, coming right at me. "You little punk!" he shouted. "You're nothing but poor white trash. You and your whole family."

A space opened in the crowd. Somebody yelled, "A fight, a fight," but Pritchett and I were too busy slugging each other to care.

At first it felt good to hit him, but Pritchett was stronger than I'd thought. Soon he was all over me, pounding my face, my stomach, my eye, my nose. I couldn't keep my guard up, I couldn't get past his. But I didn't give up. I fought like a crazy man, swinging my fists, hitting him when and wherever I could. I swear I wanted to kill Pritchett, I wanted to make him sorry he'd ever seen my face.

By the time the phys. ed. teachers shoved us apart, Pritchett's shirt was torn and his face was bloody. He was still trying to get at me, though, and I was still trying to get at him.

"Who started this?" Mr. Jackson hollered.

"Smith," Pritchett said, breathing hard. "Ask anybody."

Jackson looked at the crowd. The kids nodded. One of Pritchett's buddies said, "Smith knocked Bobby down."

"Bobby was just defending himself," another said.

Lizard started to say something, but Mr. Jackson turned to me, his muscles bulging under his suit coat. Grabbing my arm, he hustled me through the crowd and out the gym door so fast my feet didn't even touch the floor.

"Mr. Mueller will hear about this first thing Monday morning," Jackson said. "I can tell you right now he'll probably suspend you, Smith—and give you a paddling as well. In my class, you'll definitely be running laps from now till June."

Letting me go, Jackson strode back to the gym. When he opened the door, a blast of music came out—"To each his own, to each his own," one of those slow, corny songs Lizard loved so much. Probably she was dancing cheek to cheek with Pritchett again. Maybe they were laughing at me and Stu's stupid jacket. Or making jokes about my family.

I was so mad, I considered going back and punching Pritchett some more, but I figured Jackson would just throw me out again. Besides, I wasn't sure I wanted to risk Pritchett's fists. I'd expected to beat that little snot to a pulp, but I hadn't even come close. I don't know what hurt most—my eye or my pride.

"Gordy, is that you?" Toad and Doug came running toward me.

"Who do you think it is?" I asked. "Santa Claus?"

"Wow, look at your face," Toad said. "I never dreamed Pritchett could hit like that."

"Your nose is bleeding, and your eye's half shut," Doug said as if I didn't know. "You're going to have a lulu of a shiner tomorrow."

"I've had lots worse," I sneered.

Doug and Toad looked at each other. Nobody had to say it. We all knew what I meant—the old man had done quite a few fancy numbers on me in the past. Pritchett hadn't come close to matching him.

"Everyone says Mueller will suspend you, maybe even expel you," Toad said.

"Great, I hate school anyway." I wiped some of the blood away with the back of my hand. "How about Pritchett? You think he'll get suspended too?"

"A big wheel like him?" Doug flung a stone at a streetlight, missing it by a wide margin. "Fat chance."

"Mueller will probably give him a Purple Heart," Toad muttered. "You know, wounded in the line of duty."

Grumbling to ourselves, we started walking home. Overhead, the moon sailed in and out of raggedy clouds. I threw my head back and howled like a wolf. Doug and Toad joined in. When a dog started to bark, we howled even louder.

More than anything, I wished I could hop a freight and go to Oklahoma to look for Donny. If I couldn't find him, I'd just keep going. No more school. No more dumb dances. No more stupid phys. ed. teachers. Best of all, no more Lizard.

16

After Doug and Toad went home, I wandered around College Hill by myself—a lone wolf on the prowl, skulking along in the shadows, killing time till curfew. If I went back to the apartment now, Stu would see my face and know I'd been in a fight, but if I waited till eleven, he just might be asleep. By morning, maybe I'd think of a story to tell him, but I was too tired to come up with anything now.

So I kept on walking. Every time a car passed, I hid my face from the headlights. I was scared Lizard might look out the window and see me trudging along all by myself, nose bloody, jacket torn, shirt ruined. What a laugh she'd get—big bad Gordy Smith, beaten up by a jerk like Pritchett.

If I'd had any money, I would have gone to the Trolley Stoppe Shoppe to play a few rounds of pinball. Just in case I'd missed something, I searched my pockets for the hundredth time—not even a nickel for the phone, though who I'd call I didn't know.

I kicked an empty bottle so hard it flew up in the air and smashed on the pavement. Too bad I couldn't phone heaven and ask Grandma what to do. Not that I really needed to. I knew what she'd say without calling. "Go straight home and face the music"—that's what she'd have told me.

But I wasn't ready to face Stu. So I let my feet take me where they wanted, up one street and down another. Nothing can make you lonelier than being outside in the dark all by yourself, passing houses with lighted windows, glimpsing people inside, safe and warm.

By eleven-thirty, I was too cold and tired to care whether Stu was asleep or not. I tiptoed up the apartment steps and eased the door open. Stu was asleep on the couch, a poetry book facedown on his chest. He'd been waiting up for me, I guessed, and dozed off. His face was as mournful as ever.

I tiptoed past the couch, taking great care to avoid the troll's trucks and cars, and went into the bathroom. One look in the mirror told me Doug had been right about the shiner.

Wincing, I washed my face to get rid of the blood from my nose and lip, but Stu was bound to notice my eye—and my clothes, too. His jacket looked worse than I'd thought, and my one and only dress shirt was spattered with blood. I'd lost the clip-on bow tie, and the knee of my best slacks was ripped. I was really in for it.

Making no noise, I sneaked into my room, rolled Stu's jacket and my shirt into a ball, and stuffed them under my bed—way back in the corner. Barbara would probably find them someday, but at least I was safe for a while.

Just as I slid under the covers, the door opened a crack and Stu peered in. "Gordy?" he whispered.

I sighed like I was sleeping and hid my face in the pillow. Satisfied I was home, Stu shut the door. For a few minutes, he puttered around in the bathroom. Soon the toilet flushed, and I heard him go to his room. The apartment was quiet then. No one was awake but me—which made me just as lonely as I'd been outside in the dark. Maybe even lonelier.

When I finally fell asleep, I dreamed Grandma was standing beside my bed, frowning down at me. I tried to tell her how much I missed her, needed her, loved her, but the words stuck in my throat.

"What's going to become of you?" Grandma asked. "Didn't I teach you anything, Gordon?"

I tried again to speak, to say I was sorry, to promise I'd do better, but the words still wouldn't come. My voice box was busted.

Grandma turned her back. I grabbed at her old tweed coat to keep her from leaving, but she was like a cloud—a ghost made of fog and mist. I couldn't hold on to her.

"Don't go, Grandma," I called. "Don't go!"

My own voice woke me. It was six o'clock, Saturday

morning, and everybody was still asleep. Silently I slid out of bed, put on my clothes, and left the apartment. I didn't know where I'd go or what I'd do, but I still couldn't face Stu and Barbara.

I walked all over town, up and down the same streets I'd walked last night. Morning frost coated Mr. Crawford's police car windows. The newspaper still lay on the Crawfords' sidewalk. I glanced at Lizard's bedroom window. Her shades were pulled down tight. I guessed she was still sleeping, probably worn out from all that dancing with Pritchett.

While I was trudging along Route 1, I found a quarter in the gutter—the first good luck I'd had in a long time. I used it to buy a cup of coffee and two doughnuts at the Little Tavern. I sat at the counter as long as I could, sipping from the cup long after it was empty.

At ten o'clock, the library opened. I was the first person through the door. The librarian gave me a warning look, obviously remembering my last visit. I'd been with Toad and Doug, and we'd gotten a little loud. After a couple of warnings, she'd thrown us out.

Today I planned to behave myself. The library was a warm, quiet place, as small and cozy as somebody's living room. The same picture of President Roosevelt that used to hang over Grandma's radio hung over the card catalog. In the corner was an old green armchair that reminded me of one of hers—soft and kind of lumpy but comfortable. The only difference was the books, shelves and shelves of them, more than any ordinary person would ever own or read—though I'd have liked to try.

I walked up and down the aisles until I found *White Fang*. I'd already read *The Call of the Wild,* another one of Jack London's books, so I figured I'd like this one, too. I sat down in the armchair and made myself comfortable.

Although the story was good, it was hard to stay awake. The radiator hissed softly. Pages rustled. People came and went, whispering to each other. I must have dozed off because when I opened my eyes, I saw Lizard and Magpie standing a few feet away, their backs to me. Heads close together, they pulled books off the shelf, whispering and giggling.

"I thought you'd already read *Wuthering Heights,*" Magpie said.

"So? Maybe I feel like reading it again." Lizard leaned closer and whispered something in Magpie's ear.

"Oh, Heathcliff, Heathcliff." Magpie giggled. "He's *soooo* bad."

Just then Lizard looked in my direction. Hoping she hadn't seen me, I slid down in the chair and held my book in front of my face. The library was the last place on earth she'd expect to find Gordy Smith.

I heard a loud explosion of giggles. Even without lowering my book, I knew they'd spotted me.

"Look, Margaret, it knows how to read," Lizard exclaimed. "It's holding the book right side up and everything."

Magpie laughed so hard she snorted—which made her laugh and snort some more.

"It's a big thick book, too," Lizard went on in this

silly singsong voice, "with lots of long, hard words. Does it know what they all mean? Or does it have to use a dictionary?"

I kept the book in front of my face and ignored her. If Lizard saw my shiner, she'd probably run straight to Pritchett and congratulate him on the great job he'd done on me.

"Do you always hold books that close to your nose?" Lizard asked, coming closer. "Maybe you need glasses, G.A.S."

My guts felt like somebody'd tied them in knots—the usual effect Lizard had on me. "Leave me alone," I muttered. "Go bother your lover boy Pritchett."

Before I knew what she was up to, Lizard grabbed the book. "Oh, my God," she said, suddenly serious. "Your eye, Gordy, and your lip—did Bobby do that?"

"No, I fell down the steps, you stupid idiot." I got to my feet and pushed past her. Without giving her a chance to ask any more dumb questions, I left the library.

It was almost dark, that lonesome time when a person should be home with his family. The moon floated in the sky just above the treetops, and the street lamps cast a cold light. I was so hungry, I didn't know what to do—I hadn't had a thing to eat since those doughnuts.

I stopped on the corner and thought about going back to the apartment. I'd be just in time for hot dogs and beans, Barbara's idea of a Saturday night treat. But before I bit into my burned weenie, I'd have to answer a zillion questions—about my eye, my clothes, Stu's jacket, where I'd been all day.

I just wasn't up to it. Ignoring my empty stomach, I kept walking. I didn't know where I was going or what I'd do when I got there, but I figured I'd think of something.

17

ABOUT AN HOUR LATER, I HEARD SOMEONE SHOUT MY name. I turned and saw Toad and Doug running toward me.

"Where have you been all day?" Doug asked. "Stu's called our house at least three times looking for you."

"He called us, too," Toad said. "Didn't you go home last night?"

I lobbed a stone at a stop sign and hit it with a nice loud clunk. If Toad and Doug thought I'd been having a great adventure, let them go on dreaming.

"Are you running away?" Toad asked.

I shrugged. "Maybe, maybe not. It all depends on where the wind blows me."

Toad and Doug stared at me like I was some kind of hero—a guy in a western movie, roaming from one town to the next, settling scores along the way. A stranger, always alone.

"But in the meantime," I added, "I'm broke. And

hungry. How about somebody treating me to a couple of deathballs at the Little Tavern?"

Doug pulled fifty cents out of his pocket—more than enough—and gave it to me. Turning to Toad, he said, "Show Gordy what you've got in *your* pocket."

To my surprise, Toad reached into his jacket and dropped three cherry bombs into my outstretched palm. "Where did you get these?" I stared at him, truly impressed. Fireworks weren't easy to come by in Maryland.

"Uncle Herb came by the house this afternoon. He bought them in D.C., but I'm not supposed to set them off till the Fourth of July."

"That's a long time from now," I said.

Doug nodded. "Way too long."

"Firecrackers won't last till summer," I explained. "They'll blow up in your bureau drawer. Or in your pocket."

Toad stared at us. "Just like that? Without even lighting a match?"

"Haven't you ever heard of spontaneous combustion?" I asked.

"We just studied that in science, but . . ." Toad stopped and bit his lip, definitely worried. It didn't take much to scare him. "What should I do with them?"

"I've been thinking," Doug said. "What if we threw them at somebody's house? Wouldn't that scare the pants off them?"

Toad reached for the cherry bombs, but I closed them up tight in my fist. "Give them back, Gordy," he whined. "We'll get in tons of trouble if we do something like that."

"But, Toad," Doug said, "think of Donny and the toilet at the Esso station. We'll be legends like him."

Toad stuck out his lip. "They're my cherry bombs, my uncle gave them to me, and I want them back."

"Do what you like, Auntie Toad," I said. "Go home or come with us, but we're keeping the cherry bombs."

While Toad whined and moaned and fussed, Doug and I tried to decide whose house to hit. Pritchett's was my number one choice. But just when I almost had Doug convinced, a door opened and somebody yelled, "You boys put one foot on my property and I'll call the cops."

We'd been so busy arguing we hadn't noticed we were standing in front of Whitman's house. Doug looked at me and I looked at him. Giving a loud whoop, the three of us ran down the streetcar tracks. The crazy professor would be our victim.

"He'll know you did it, Gordy," Toad said. "He blames everything on you, even stuff you didn't do."

Toad was right. Ever since I'd hit him in the mouth with a snowball, Whitman had been calling Stu and accusing me of evil deeds I'd almost always had nothing to do with. I'd trampled his rare azalea bushes, for instance. I'd broken a branch off his precious French lilac. I'd made a crank phone call. He even swore I'd stolen his wife's underwear off the clothesline.

I wasn't guilty of any of those things except maybe breaking that stupid branch, which was totally accidental. But as far as Whitman was concerned, I was Smith the bad guy, Smith the juvenile delinquent, Smith the kid he wanted shot on sight.

"Like Doug said, we'll be legends," I told Toad. "Nobody's ever forgotten the day Donny blew up the toilet at the Esso station. They won't forget us, either."

Though I didn't say it, I was thinking about Lizard. She'd hear about the cherry bombs. Maybe she'd be impressed. Maybe she wouldn't. Maybe it didn't make any difference. Like everybody else in College Hill, Lizard thought I was a rotten, no-good kid. Stealing records, fighting, getting thrown out of the dance, disappearing all day, throwing cherry bombs—I was heading for reform school right behind Donny, and I couldn't have cared less. Hadn't everybody always known I'd end up there? Maybe I'd finally make Stu happy and end up a well-adjusted crook.

"Let's go to the Little Tavern first," Toad said, still stalling. "You said you were hungry, Gordy. I wouldn't mind having a deathball myself. As a matter of fact, I—"

"My belly's not as important to me as yours is to you." I poked the flab around Toad's waist. "The Little Tavern can wait."

With Toad complaining every step of the way, we sneaked back to the Whitmans' house. A light shone from the kitchen window, but the rest of the place was dark.

"Let's see what he's doing," I whispered.

The three of us crept down the driveway and peered into the kitchen. Whitman sat at the table playing solitaire. A bottle of Lord Calvert whiskey, the old man's favorite, stood at his elbow, and there was a glass next to it. Every now and then, he took a sip from the glass. Mrs. Whitman was washing dishes, her back to us. And to him, too.

"He looks kind of sad," Toad said. "Maybe we should just leave him be."

"I've got no pity for drunks," I muttered.

"He's not like your dad," Toad said. "He—"

"What do you mean?" I glared at Toad. In the light from the kitchen window, his face was as pale and round as the man in the moon. "Are you saying it's okay for a rich guy to hit the bottle? But not a bum like my old man?"

That confused Toad. "No, Gordy, I just—"

"Can it, you guys," Doug said. "We're here to throw some cherry bombs, not get into a dumb argument."

"All I meant was—"

"Shut up, Toad," I hissed, "or I'll kick your fat behind from here to next Sunday."

Toad scowled, but he had enough sense to hunker down beside Doug and keep quiet.

"I'll hold the storm door open," Doug said, "and Gordy can throw the cherry bombs into the vestibule. They'll go off with a really big bang in a little space like that."

For a second, I thought about asking Doug how come I was the one throwing the cherry bombs and he was the one holding the door. But then I decided I'd be the true hero, the guy who did the actual deed, who took the biggest risk. Doug would just be my sidekick.

Toad frowned. "How about me? They're my cherry bombs. Don't I get to do anything?"

"I thought you didn't want to be involved," Doug said.

"Well, now that I'm here," Toad muttered, "I might as well have some fun."

"You can be the lookout," I said. "Go hide in the bushes and yell if you see anything."

"Like what?"

Doug sighed. "Use your imagination, Toad."

"Listen up," I whispered. "This is a sneak attack, a raid, like the old days when we played war. As soon as I throw the cherry bombs, everybody run. We'll meet up at the Little Tavern."

The three of us shook hands and slapped each other on the back. Three musketeers, buddies forever, "one for all and all for one"—that was us.

After Toad disappeared into a clump of fancy evergreens, Doug and I crept around the corner of the house and tiptoed up the back porch steps. I waited till Doug eased the storm door open. Then I lit the cherry bombs and threw them.

As Doug predicted, the cherry bombs exploded with a deafening blast. A second later, the porch light flashed on and the door flew open. Whitman yelled my name, following it with a string of curses. Dogs barked.

I turned to run, but I tripped over a little bush and fell flat on my face. It knocked the wind clean out of me. The next thing I knew, the professor had an arm-lock on me. I struggled to get away, but he was pretty strong for an old guy.

"There's no use putting up a fight," Whitman snarled. "My wife's calling the police. I hope they haul you to jail and throw away the key."

He yanked me to my feet and shoved me up the steps and into the kitchen. Before the door slammed shut, I looked over my shoulder. No sign of Doug or Toad. My buddies were probably home already, hiding under their beds for fear I'd tell on them.

Well, Gordy Smith was made of finer stuff than that. Even if his buddies betrayed him, he'd be true to them.

18

THE PROFESSOR SLAMMED ME DOWN IN A CHAIR AT THE kitchen table and told me not to move. While he hollered about mayhem and destruction, his wife leaned against the sink and gazed at me like she wasn't sure what to think. The room was hot, the light bright, and I was so hungry my stomach was growling almost as loud as the professor was yelling.

Just when it seemed things couldn't get worse, Mr. Crawford arrived in full cop uniform—badge, gun, and everything.

I stared at Lizard's dad and he stared at me. Just thinking of what she must have told him about me made me feel sick. No doubt he'd be happy to haul me off to jail. Why let a beast like me roam the streets? As long as I was loose, the good citizens of College Hill weren't safe in their own houses.

"What's going on, Roland?" Crawford asked.

Whitman immediately launched into a long, rambling tirade about the cherry bombs and all the other stuff he thought I'd done, including the theft of his wife's underwear.

When the professor stopped to take a breath, Crawford turned to me. "Is this true, Gordon?"

"Not all of it," I said. "I never stole anybody's underwear." I was trying to sound tough, even wisecrack a little, but my voice came out as high as a girl's.

"What about the cherry bombs?" Crawford asked.

I gnawed on my thumbnail. It made no sense to lie. Whitman had practically caught me red-handed. "It was just a joke," I muttered.

"A joke?" Whitman turned on me, his face purple. "You call that a *joke*? You could've burned my house down, you miserable little anarchist!"

"Now, Roland," Crawford said, "let me handle this."

Whitman poured himself another glass of whiskey. Didn't even add water. I glanced at Mrs. Whitman. Twisting a dish towel nervously, she watched her husband sip the whiskey. I had a feeling she wished he'd put the bottle away before Crawford arrived.

Crawford stepped closer to me. His holster creaked as he leaned across the table and stared into my eyes. "Where did you get the cherry bombs, Gordon? You know as well as I do they're illegal in Maryland."

I gnawed my thumbnail harder. I was down to the quick now, and I tasted blood. "Maybe I found them."

"Do you expect me to believe that?" Crawford shoved his face even nearer. "Who gave them to you?"

"I bought them in D.C.," I said, avoiding his eyes,

which were just as blue as Lizard's, the color of the sky in October. "They're legal there."

"Not to a minor," Crawford snapped. "Tell me who sold them to you and maybe we can work out a deal with the professor. Get you out of this mess."

"It was just some guy on a corner," I told him, making up my story as I went along. "He gave them to me for a quarter. I guess he needed money."

Crawford sighed and turned to Whitman. "What do you want me to do with this boy?"

Whitman knocked back the rest of his whiskey and reached for the bottle. "Haul him off to jail, lock him up, throw away the key."

"Roland, you know I can't do that." Crawford took the bottle and handed it to Mrs. Whitman, who scurried away with it like she was running for a touchdown. If she had any sense, she'd pour it down the toilet. I'd gotten rid of the old man's liquor that way more than once. Of course he'd beaten me black and blue later, but in a way it was worth it.

"Are you going to press charges?" Crawford asked.

"Possession of fireworks," Whitman said, counting my crimes on his fingers, "disturbing the peace, destruction of property, trespassing—that little miscreant is guilty as sin."

"Gordon may have disturbed the peace," Crawford said, "and he certainly trespassed, but I can't see that he destroyed anything. Why don't we forget the whole thing?"

"Forget?"

"Give the boy another chance, Roland. I'm sure he'll—"

"Give him another chance?" Once more Whitman's face turned purple. "So he can burn my house to the ground next time? Trample my shrubbery? Ruin my lawn?"

"I've talked to Gordon's brother. He says—"

"*He* says—isn't his brother the coward who deserted during the war? The bum my former neighbors' daughter married?"

"Stuart's a responsible young man now," Crawford said. "He's promised—"

"I don't give a whoop-de-do about any deserter's promises!"

Things went on like that for quite a while. I couldn't believe Crawford was actually taking up for me and Stu. Maybe Lizard hadn't said as much bad stuff about me as I'd thought.

It was Mrs. Whitman who finally settled it. Though she hadn't said a word all night, she stepped up to her husband, looked him in the eye, and said, "Roland, the truth is, you're in no shape to decide anything. I suggest you go to bed and sleep it off. In the morning, when you can think straight, we'll talk it over."

The professor scowled, but he didn't hit her the way the old man would have hit Mama if she had dared speak up like that. "I am tired," he admitted. "Hazel's right, it's late. We should all go to bed."

Crawford took my arm and led me toward the door. "I'll drive Gordon home," he told the professor. "Call the station when you decide what you want to do. But don't be too hard on the boy."

Keeping a tight grip on me, Crawford shoved me into the police car. "Where were you all day, Gordon? Stuart's been worried to death."

"No place special." I was tired and hungry, and I wasn't in the mood to answer any questions. What I would have liked most of all was to be home in bed.

"Elizabeth told me she saw you at the library this afternoon," Crawford said.

"Maybe I like to read," I muttered. "Maybe I'm not as dumb as Lizard thinks."

"Lizard?" For a second, Crawford looked puzzled. Then the light dawned. "Do you mean Elizabeth?"

"She's probably told you a bunch of lies about me—how stupid I am, how rude I am, how bad I am. She *hates* me. Loathes me. Despises me. Just ask her. She'll tell you."

"Is that right?" For some reason Crawford seemed to think what I'd said was funny. "I must admit we hear a lot about you at the dinner table. Too much, as a matter of fact. Gordy this, Gordy that. I'd like to get through one meal without hearing your name."

"None of what she says is true," I mumbled. "Not one word."

"Was Elizabeth lying about the fight you and Bobby Pritchett had at the dance?"

I toyed with the zipper on my jacket, running it up

and down till it got stuck halfway. "We had a little disagreement," I admitted.

"Is that how you got the black eye?"

"Maybe," I said, remembering the lies Mama had taught me. "Then again, maybe I fell down the steps. Maybe I walked into a door. Maybe I—"

"Let me tell you something," Crawford cut in. "You're not half as tough as you pretend to be. Right now you're scared to death."

I shook my head, trying to keep up my act, but Crawford wasn't finished reading my mind.

"If you're not scared, you should be," he went on. "Whitman's a nice guy when he's sober, but after he gets a few whiskeys under his belt, he's nobody to fool with. You better pray he forgets about those firecrackers. If he presses charges, you could end up doing a couple of months in reform school."

I went back to biting my nails. Reform school—that would just about kill Stu. Wouldn't do much for me, either. Donny had told me plenty of stories about his six months there. Getting beat up by guys twice his size wasn't the worst of it.

Crawford pulled into the apartment parking lot and cut the engine. "I'd be willing to bet you had some accomplices tonight," he said. "Tommy Sutcliffe and Doug Murray come to mind."

I let Toad's and Doug's names drop into the silence like stones. If Crawford thought I'd betray my buddies, he was wrong. Even though they'd deserted me, I didn't plan to save myself by blabbing on them.

When I didn't say anything, Crawford cleared his throat. "Listen to me, Gordy. You're not stupid. Use your brains once in a while. Behave yourself."

A gust of wind struck the side of the car and rocked it. Down the track, a train whistle blew. I felt like telling Crawford to pass the news about my brains to his daughter. She'd laugh in his face.

A few seconds passed, maybe a minute. Crawford sighed and opened the car door. "Well, there's no sense keeping your brother waiting."

I followed him toward the apartment building. The light was on in our living room, and I saw someone look out. Stu must have waited up for me. Soon I'd have to face the music, as Grandma would have said.

19

WHEN CRAWFORD RAISED HIS HAND TO KNOCK ON OUR door, it flew open and June came running out, followed by the troll.

"Gordy, Gordy!" June wrapped her skinny little arms around me, and her head banged into my chest so hard she almost knocked me over. The troll hopped from one foot to the other, babbling about bad Yuncle Poopoo.

"Where have you been, Gordy?" Stu's face was pale, worried, almost scared. "I've been all over town looking for you."

At the same time, Barbara said, "Your eye—oh, Gordy, what happened to your eye? And your lip—it's cut, too."

June clung to me. "I thought you went off and left me, I thought you weren't coming back, I thought I'd never see you again, I thought—" She was crying too hard to finish the sentence.

"Don't be silly," I muttered, secretly pleased she was making such a fuss over me. "I wouldn't go anywhere without you, June Bug."

Barbara gave me a hug. "I saved a hot dog for you. It's cold by now, but I bet you haven't eaten a thing all day."

I was too surprised to answer. The way I'd acted, I hadn't expected Barbara to offer me food. I opened my mouth to thank her, but she was already leading June and Brent to bed.

"Is Whitman pressing charges?" Stu asked Crawford.

"When he sobers up, he may decide it's not worth pursuing. But on the other hand—" Crawford shrugged. "Whitman's hard to predict."

Stu looked about as glum as a man can look, but he reached out and shook Crawford's hand. "Thanks for bringing Gordy home," he said. "I'll make sure he stays here for a while."

Crawford eyeballed me and then turned to Stu. "Gordon's not a bad kid," he said. "I've seen lots worse, believe me."

The door shut behind him. "I'm sorry, Stu," I said. "I didn't think—"

"That's just it," he said wearily. "You didn't think. You *never* think."

"I know, you're right, I never think." I was so tired I'd have agreed with anything Stu said. But it was true—I never thought, at least not straight. My head was full of ideas, but they were all jumbled, some urging me to do one thing, others urging me to do the opposite. It was like trying to tune in a radio station during a thunderstorm—nothing came in but static.

"Tell me about it," Stu said wearily. "Start at the beginning."

"Can't we go to bed?" I asked. "In the morning, things might not seem so bad. They might—"

"I want to hear it now." Stu sat down at the dining table, and I took a seat opposite him. Between us was a sloppy heap of books and papers so high I could barely see over it.

"Well," I said slowly, "it all started when I asked Lizard to the Sweetheart Dance and she turned me down." I went on from there, telling Stu pretty much everything except for stealing the record album—no sense making things even worse for myself.

"It's this town," I finished up. "Nobody likes us here. They make cracks about you and the old man. Call you a deserter, call him a drunk."

Stu chewed his lower lip, but he didn't say a word. The clock ticked, the refrigerator cut on and off—monotonous sounds you hear everywhere.

"It was different at Grandma's," I said. "She made sure people treated us right. She took up for us. She *cared.*"

Stu looked startled. "I care about you, Gordy."

"No, you don't." I waved my hand at the table. "Books—that's what's important to you, that's all that matters. You keep your head buried in them like an ostrich, just hoping nobody will bother you. It's not me you care about, it's your dumb education."

"That's not fair, Gordy. It isn't even true." Stu peered over the books, his face tight with worry. "Our whole future depends on my graduating and getting a job. Can't you understand that?"

I snorted. "You think teaching English is going to make you rich?"

"I don't want to be rich," Stu went on. "I want to do something important with my life, and teaching—well, teaching seems like the best way to—"

Red-faced, Stu ground to a stop, as if he'd just revealed some deep, dark secret about himself. "Does that sound pompous?" he asked, looking even more worried than usual.

"How should I know?" I scowled at him, annoyed at the way he threw fancy words around. Was he trying to make me feel stupid?

"Never mind." Stu sighed as if I was too dumb to understand.

Suddenly fed up, I jumped to my feet. "Why don't you say what you're really thinking? Why don't you cuss and yell and call me a stupid, no-good juvenile delinquent? Why don't you haul off and punch me?"

My voice rose with every word, but Stu just sat there looking at me. "Yelling doesn't solve anything," he said in a maddeningly calm voice. "Neither does swearing or hitting. I should think you'd know that as well as I do, Gordy."

I lost every shred of patience. How could he be so blind, so bullheaded, so smug? It was beyond belief. "Who do you think you are?" I yelled. "Saint Stuart?"

"All I want is a nice home, a decent place where nobody fights or loses his temper!" Stu's face reddened, and his voice began to rise, too. "Why can't you understand, Gordy? Why can't you help?"

"Help you live in some dreamworld?" It was all I could do not to punch his stupid face. "The only way I can do that is leave, go out to Tulsa, and find Donny. He hasn't gone to college, he's not smart like you, but he's no chump. He knows a lot more about life than you ever will!"

Before Stu could stop me, I swept everything off the table—books, papers, pencils and pens, a coffee cup. "There," I shouted, daring him to do something about it. "That's what I think of you and your books!"

Stu ran around the table and grabbed me. "Stop it, Gordy, stop it!" he yelled.

"Make me, you coward, you yellow deserter!" I struggled to get away from him, I cussed, kicked, hit. I wanted to throw more stuff, smash things, fight. If I could have, I would've hurled the typewriter out the window.

Barbara ran into the room. "Stu, Gordy, what are you doing?" she cried. "Have you gone crazy? For God's sake, stop it!"

Stu let go of me so suddenly I reeled backward. "It's like Davis Road all over again," he shouted. "I'll never escape from that house, never! Yelling, swearing, fighting—why does he behave like this? I've done all I can. Why can't he at least try?"

While Stu ranted and raved, Barbara stared at me,

her face bewildered. Unable to meet her eyes, I tried to breathe normally. My heart was pounding so hard, I thought it might burst. I'd done what I wanted, I'd made Stu lose his temper, I'd made him see the real me, but I felt worse instead of better. Without looking at anybody, I started picking up the books. There'd been just enough coffee in the cup to spill on some of Stu's papers and ruin them. Barbara would have to type them over.

Suddenly ashamed, I knelt on the floor, half hidden by the table, and tried not to cry. Now Stu knew me for what I was—a worthless, rotten kid, just as bad as everyone thought. I'd never be the well-adjusted boy he wanted me to be. Like Whitman said, Crawford should've hauled me off to jail and thrown away the key. It was what I deserved.

I got to my feet slowly and laid the pile of paper on the table. "I'm sorry," I muttered. "Honest. I didn't mean what I said."

"Yes, you did," Stu said. "You meant every damn word of it."

I looked at my brother and saw Mama, dejected, beaten down, miserable. But then he raised his head and looked me in the eye, and he wasn't Mama after all.

"Some of what you said was true," he said calmly, "and some of it wasn't. You're my brother, Gordy. I love you, you're important to me. But so is college. It's my way of fighting back. It's proof I won't end up like Pop."

I looked at Stu, too surprised to say anything. I'd never dreamed he worried about following in our father's footsteps. They were cut from different cloth, Stu and the old man. But Donny and me—we were a pretty close match.

"Or Mama either," Stu added, just as if he was reading my mind. "I want to leave Davis Road behind. I want our lives to be different."

Barbara put her arms around Stu, and he clung to her for a second. If I'd been a few years younger, I'd have hugged her myself, but I was too big for that kind of stuff now.

"I don't know about you two," Barbara said, "but I'm exhausted. Let's go to bed."

"You go ahead," Stu told her. "I have an English exam Monday, and I haven't had much time to study."

Barbara took the book out of Stu's hands. "No," she said firmly. "You've studied enough."

For once Stu gave in. Maybe he was just too tired to argue. At any rate, he followed Barbara down the hall to their bedroom, and I went to mine.

I thought I'd fall asleep the minute my head touched the pillow, but I ended up lying awake a long time, thinking about the old man. He might be in California, but part of him was still with me, sitting on my shoulder, tempting me to fight, cuss, yell. The devil himself, that's who he was. And no amount of studying was going to make him go away. There weren't enough books in the world to wall him out of my life.

20

IT RAINED ALL DAY SUNDAY—A LONG DREARY DAY WITH nothing to do but read and listen to the radio. Not that it mattered. I wasn't allowed to leave the apartment anyway.

Night came and went, and Monday arrived right on schedule. No atom bombs fell while I slept, I didn't wake up with polio, the school neither blew up nor burned down. There was nothing to do but get dressed and walk to the streetcar stop. Like it or not, I'd have to face Mueller.

Toad and Doug were waiting for me, looking a little ashamed, I thought, but not nearly enough.

"What happened at the professor's house?" Toad asked. "We didn't want to run off and leave you there, but—"

"There was nothing we could do, Gordy," Doug added quickly. "Not after he dragged you inside."

I shoved my hands into my pockets and shrugged.

"Whitman was full of crap, but Crawford calmed him down."

Toad stared at me. "*Lizard* was there?"

"Her *father,* you dope," I said. "The cop."

Doug sneered. "You're so dumb, Auntie Toad."

"Don't call me that," Toad whined.

Doug gave him a little shove. "I'll call you anything I want, Auntie Toad."

The idiots started quarreling like kindergartners. They made me sick. When the streetcar came, I got on first and sat down next to an old lady who gave me a suspicious look. Maybe she thought I was going to steal her purse or something.

Toad stopped beside me. "Aren't you sitting with me and Doug?"

I didn't answer. Jerks—always setting me up and leaving me to take the blame. And then acting like it was nothing for me to be sore at. No need to apologize.

"What's bothering you, Gordo?" Doug asked. "If you think we told—"

Without looking at him, I opened my English book and started reading a dumb poem about some poor chump wandering as lonely as a cloud. I knew what the poet meant—clouds can look pretty lonesome sometimes, floating around in the sky all by themselves, small and gray and sad.

"Sit down, boys," the driver said. "You're holding up the show."

"Oh, leave him be. Let him sulk. Who cares." Doug pushed Toad down the aisle to the seat in the back where we usually sat. I could hear them laughing. Let them. Who cared.

When the streetcar stopped at Garfield Road, Lizard and Magpie got on with some other kids. I kept on reading about dopey daffodils fluttering and dancing in the breeze. Cornball stuff, but it saved me from looking at Lizard. I wondered how much she knew about my little visit with her father and the professor—and if she'd told anyone else.

At Cherry Road, Pritchett and his friends boarded in a group, laughing and talking. I felt like sticking my foot out and tripping Pritchett as he passed me, but the pleasure of seeing him fall wasn't worth getting kicked off the streetcar. He didn't notice me anyhow. What bothered me most was he didn't have a mark on his face. Not one. All I'd done was bloody his ugly nose. But look at me—I could hardly see out of my left eye. It wasn't fair.

A few seconds later Pritchett said hello to Lizard. Though I couldn't hear what she said, he must not have liked it because he muttered, "Be that way, Lizzy. See if I care."

I glanced over my shoulder. Pritchett had moved to a seat near the back of the streetcar. While he joked with his friends, Lizard whispered to Magpie. She caught my eye and leaned even closer to Magpie. If I knew them, they'd soon start laughing like hyenas.

To spare myself the agony, I turned around and went on reading the dumb daffodil poem. It was just the kind of thing Mrs. Ianotti would give a test on.

I walked to school from the streetcar by myself. Not that Toad and Doug seemed to care. Maybe they were tired of me, too. On the school steps, Lizard and Magpie passed me. They both stared hard at me, but neither said a word, just rushed on by like they were in a big hurry to go somewhere.

In homeroom, Miss Sparks called roll, and then we saluted the flag and said the Lord's Prayer. At any minute I expected to be called to the office, but the bell rang for first period without anyone coming to get me. I went to math, where I learned I'd gotten a D on the quiz we'd had last week, and then on to English. I was beginning to think Jackson hadn't reported me after all. Maybe he'd forgotten all about the fight.

I opened my grammar book, but it was harder than usual to keep my mind on it. My thoughts kept drifting—was Mueller going to call me to the office or not?

All around me, pages turned and pencils scratched on paper. Kids coughed, their desks creaked. Mrs. Ianotti droned on and on about gerunds and participles and other boring things. My thoughts drifted further and further away. Why was Lizard mad at Pritchett? Had he gotten fresh with her after the dance? Couldn't blame him for trying—if I ever got Lizard alone and in a friendly mood, I'd give her a squeeze or two myself.

Stupid thought—that kiss I'd sneaked in the snow was probably the only one I'd ever get from Lizzy Lizard. I'd ruined my chances with her a long time ago, starting in kindergarten when I pulled her hair every chance I got. It was so pretty, I couldn't keep my hands off it.

"Gordon Smith!" Mrs. Ianotti shouted. "Do you know the answer or not?"

I stared at her, too startled to do more than shake my head. I'd been thinking so hard, I hadn't even heard the question.

"I would appreciate it if you would pay attention, Gordon." Mrs. Ianotti's voice was cold enough to freeze a person's blood. "You may not realize it, but a thorough knowledge of grammar is essential if one wishes to succeed in this world."

"Yes, ma'am," I mumbled.

Behind me, a couple of smart-aleck girls giggled as Mrs. Ianotti made a little mark in her grade book. Then she called on Jimmy Watson, who was waving his hand so hard I hoped it would fall off.

Jimmy knew both the question and the answer. He always did. If Mrs. Ianotti was right about knowing whether your particles dangled or not, he'd go far in the world. And I wouldn't. Tough for me and good-o for Jimmy.

Just before the bell rang for third period, a student aide appeared at the door and gave Mrs. Ianotti a yellow slip. She read it and called me to her desk. "Mr. Mueller wants to see you in his office, Gordon," she said without a speck of emotion.

Behind me, a ripple ran through the class, but I paid no attention. I knew what I'd done. No terrible news waited for me in the principal's office this time.

Except for me and the prissy senior girl who'd come to fetch me, the hall was empty. Neither her saddle oxfords nor my basketball shoes made any noise. All the classroom doors were shut, but the silence wouldn't last long. In about two minutes, the bell would ring and kids would fill the halls. I picked up my pace—no sense being seen with a student aide. Everybody would know exactly where she was taking me.

When I walked into Mueller's office, I got the shock of my life. Pritchett and his mother were sitting next to each other on one side of the desk. Across from them was Barbara. Mr. Jackson leaned against a wall, his arms folded across his chest. The tension was so thick I could hardly breathe.

Mueller frowned when he saw me. "Sit down beside your sister-in-law, Smith."

I did as he asked. To my surprise, Barbara gave my hand a quick squeeze. "Where's Stu?" I whispered.

"Taking an exam," Barbara whispered back, pressing a finger to her lips to shut me up.

Mueller leaned back in his chair and let his eyes roam around the room, taking us all in. The scene reminded me of a movie I'd seen once where a detective gathered all the murder suspects together and proved which one did it. Only in this case everybody already knew the guilty party—Gordon Peter Smith, aka G.A.S. and Yuncle Poopoo.

Like Jackson, I folded my arms and looked Mueller straight in the eye. Let him paddle me in front of everyone. I wouldn't even whimper.

Mueller cleared his throat. "I've brought you together because I've received several conflicting reports about the incident at the Sweetheart Dance. Frankly, I want to get to the bottom of the matter."

Turning to Pritchett, he said. "You first. Tell me what happened."

"Yes, sir," Pritchett said, pink-cheeked and eager to report. "I was dancing with Elizabeth Crawford, she was my date, and Gordon Smith deliberately bumped into me. He tried to knock me down, sir."

"It's not the first time the Smith boy has bothered Bobby," Old Lady Pritchett put in. "He pushed him in the cafeteria and made him spill spaghetti sauce all over a good pair of trousers, utterly ruining them. Five dollars—that's what it cost me to replace them."

Mr. Mueller shot her a look from under those bushy eyebrows of his. "Please let Bobby give his own account, Roberta."

Pritchett glanced at his mother. If I hadn't hated him so much, I'd have pitied him. You'd think the poor jerk couldn't speak for himself.

"Sorry, Mike," Mrs. Pritchett said. "I didn't mean to interrupt, I just wanted—"

Mueller turned back to Pritchett. "What happened next?"

Pritchett shrugged. "A little while later, Smith threw a punch at me. He was cursing and carrying on like a crazy man. I had to defend myself, sir."

"You know what sort of home the Smith boy comes from, Mike," Mrs. Pritchett added, earning another dirty look from Pritchett. I bet he was dying to tell her to shut up. Anybody could see she was making things worse for him.

"Gordon's father was an alcoholic," Mrs. Pritchett went on. "One brother spent some time in reform school, and the other deserted during the war."

Barbara opened her mouth to speak, but Mueller motioned her to be quiet. "You did nothing to provoke Gordon, Bobby?"

"Well, I might have teased him a little." Pritchett shot me a look of pure disgust. "A person ought to be able to take a joke."

"And what do you call a joke, Bobby?" Mueller asked.

"I don't remember exactly what I said, sir," Pritchett said. "But it was all in fun."

Mueller picked up a sheet of notebook paper and read, "First Bobby made some cracks about Gordy's jacket, then he started insulting his family, saying mean things about Stuart and Gordy's father. It was like he wanted Gordy to hit him, and when he did, Bobby really hurt Gordy. He kept hitting him and hitting him and hitting him. It was horrible. Mr. Jackson blamed it all on Gordy and threw him out of the dance, but he should have thrown Bobby out too. It was his fault, not Gordy's."

"Whoever wrote that is a liar," Pritchett said. "Like I told you, sir, I was defending myself. Smith is nothing but a troublemaker and everybody knows it. I—"

Good old Mrs. Pritchett cut in again. "Surely you

wouldn't take the word of a tattletale against Bobby. You've known him since he was a baby, Mike. We've gone to the same church, had the same friends, played bridge together—"

"Roberta," Mueller said, "will you please be quiet?"

Old Lady Pritchett drew in her breath so hard it's a wonder there was any air left for the rest of us to breathe. "Why did you ask me to come if you expected me to sit here silently and listen to you malign my son?"

"I invited both you and Mrs. Smith to be here so there would be no misunderstandings." Mueller leaned toward me. "Gordon, did Bobby insult your family at the dance, or did a friend of yours write this to save your hide?"

"I don't have any idea who wrote it, sir." It was true. While Mueller had been talking, I'd been chewing my thumbnail and trying to figure out who liked me enough to send a note to the principal. It couldn't have been Toad or Doug. They were too afraid of getting into trouble themselves to go out on a limb for me. Was it possible I had a secret admirer? Ha—pretty unlikely.

"But are the allegations valid?" Mueller asked. "Did Bobby provoke you?"

I shrugged. "I don't remember." There was no way on God's green earth I'd rat on anybody, not even Pritchett.

Mr. Mueller sighed loudly. "How can boys so young be afflicted with such severe memory loss?" Turning to Jackson, he said, "What do you think, Earl?"

Jackson shifted his weight from one foot to the

other. "I must admit I blamed Smith for the fight initially, mainly because of his attitude in my class. He's uncooperative. Mouthy. A poor team player." He shifted his weight back again. "But I might have misjudged—I didn't see how it started."

Pritchett stared at Jackson, obviously surprised. "Smith started it, sir. Ask anybody."

"This is ridiculous," Mrs. Pritchett said. I thought Pritchett was going to kick her if she didn't shut up, but he restrained himself. "We all know what sort of boy Gordon is," she went on. "But Bobby comes from a good home, a fine family. *He's* not a troublemaker."

"We seem to be overlooking something," Mueller went on. "Take a good look at Gordon's face, Roberta. Your son—who is both taller and heavier—gave him that black eye and those bruises."

The old bag's skin flushed all the way down to her fingertips. "Gordon's brother probably did that. It's no secret their father beat the whole family. The apple never falls far from the tree, you know."

That was all Barbara could take. Turning to Mrs. Pritchett, she said, "If you think you can sit there and insult my husband, you have another think coming! Stu has never laid a hand on anyone in his entire life. Violence of any sort is totally and utterly repugnant to him."

"Don't you dare speak to me like that," Mrs. Pritchett said. "I used to play bridge with your mother. What she would think of your behavior I cannot imagine! I swear you're as common as any Smith now."

"Good for me," Barbara said, her face scarlet.

"All right, ladies, all right. I've heard enough." Mueller got to his feet and ran a hand through his hair. "Gordon and Bobby, I'm suspending both of you for three days. When you return to school on Thursday, you will have two weeks of detention in my office. Three-thirty to four-thirty. Be sure and bring plenty of homework."

"But, sir," Pritchett said, "I'll miss basketball practice."

"I'm aware of that," Mueller said. "Mr. Jackson and I have decided to remove you from the team for the rest of the season. A boy with a temper like yours has no place in varsity sports."

"That's not fair!" Pritchett bellowed.

To tell the truth, I was just as surprised as Pritchett. I'd expected to be blamed for everything—like Toad had said, Pritchett would get a Purple Heart and I'd be sent to reform school. But Mueller had been fair. Neither Pritchett nor I had dreamed of such a possibility.

By then, Mueller had had enough of all of us. Ignoring Mrs. Pritchett's protests, he shooed us out the door as if we were a bunch of squalling cats. Miss Greenbaum busied herself typing as we swept past, but the student aide stared goggle-eyed. I bet she could hardly wait to go to her next class and tell everybody Pritchett had been suspended and wouldn't be sinking any baskets for a while. That was definitely N-E-W-S.

21

BARBARA AND I LEFT SCHOOL TOGETHER. ONCE I WOULD'VE been glad to be out of class at eleven o'clock, but not today. Not with Barbara looking even glummer than I felt.

Even though I didn't always see eye to eye with her, I liked Barbara and I wanted her to like me. Now she was mad at me. And who could blame her? She'd had to leave Brent with Mrs. Reilly and come all the way down here on the streetcar just to hear Old Lady Pritchett insult Stu and her both. And all because of me, Gordon P. Smith.

"I'm sorry I put you to so much trouble," I told her, meaning every word of it. "First the professor and now this—I don't blame you for being sore."

Barbara didn't answer right away, didn't look at me either. At first I thought she was giving me the silent treatment. Either that or she hadn't heard me—apologizing didn't come easy for me, so I hadn't spoken very loud.

Suddenly she turned to me. "Who does Mrs. Pritchett think she is? The way she talked to me—I wanted to slap her face! And that son of hers—the big bully. He must be half a foot taller than you, Gordy."

"Maybe I'm shorter than Pritchett," I said, "but I'm just as tough as he is. Maybe even tougher." I punched the air with my fists. Did she think I was Pritchett's helpless victim? "Just let him start something, I'll finish it, I'll—"

Barbara stopped in midstride, grabbed my shoulders, and whirled me around to face her. "If you ever get into another fight with Bobby Pritchett," she said. "I'll put you under house arrest till you're twenty-one years old!"

For the next five minutes, she read me the riot act from A to Z—no more fighting, no more staying out late, no more cherry bombs. She even got in a few licks about Stu's jacket, which she'd found under my bed. My grades had to improve, she said, especially math. My attitude, too.

"You go around with this ugly look on your face," she said. "You blow up at every little thing. What's bothering you, Gordy? Why are you so mad all the time?"

I pulled away from Barbara and kicked a stone hard enough to send it bouncing down the sidewalk. Grandma had asked me the same question a long time ago. I hadn't had a good answer then and I didn't have one now. I guessed that meant I hadn't changed much. Gordy Smith—as mad as ever, as mean as ever, as ugly as ever, as dumb as ever.

"Is it your father you're mad at?" Barbara asked, her voice softer now. "Your mother? The whole world?"

Yes to all three, but what was I supposed to do about it? Mama couldn't help being the way she was. Getting mad at her made no sense. And the old man was gone, I'd never see him again—spilled milk, water under the bridge, that's all he was. No sense being mad at him, no sense being mad at the world either. Nobody in College Hill was going to change. It was stupid to think they would. To them, I'd always be poor white trash from Davis Road.

Anger rose in my throat as bitter as bile. I spat hard, shooting the stuff between my teeth the way Donny had taught me, but I couldn't get rid of the taste. No matter what I did, that anger would always be there, ticking away in my head like a bomb.

"Sometimes I think Stu's just as mad as you are," Barbara said, "but he bottles it all up inside, worries, gets depressed, won't admit what's really bothering him. At the rate he's going, he'll end up with ulcers."

A gust of wind blew her hair forward, hiding her face. We'd reached the corner of Route 1, and the traffic light was red. Cars and trucks rumbled past, making so much noise we couldn't talk without yelling.

When the signal changed, we crossed the highway and turned down a side road leading to the streetcar stop. It was quiet there. The houses reminded me of

Grandma's—towers on the side, front porches, fancy trim, shutters, tall trees, big yards. Not a person in sight at this time of day. Kids were in school, husbands at work, mothers inside, cleaning or doing the laundry, maybe listening to soap operas on the radio while they ironed, like William's mother.

I didn't realize Barbara had been crying until she sniffed and wiped her eyes with her coat sleeve like a little kid.

I touched her arm. "I won't go near the professor's house," I promised. "And I'll stay away from Pritchett, too."

Barbara sniffed again. "I don't want to see or hear from his mother again. I couldn't stand her when I was little and I can't stand her now. If you want to know the truth, my mother hated those bridge parties. She thought Mrs. Pritchett was a spiteful old gossip."

"The apple never falls far from the tree, you know," I said, mimicking Mrs. Pritchett's la-di-da voice.

That made Barbara laugh.

When we got to the stop, we sat on the railing and waited for the next streetcar to come around the bend. It was a cloudy day, but the wind had a soft edge. I unzipped my jacket and relaxed. Spring was coming. You could feel it in the air.

Barbara sighed and tipped her head back to look at the sky. "I must admit it's nice to be away from that typewriter for a while. My fingertips are getting numb—not to mention my rear end."

Numb or not, Barbara had a nice rear end, but I knew

better than to tell her that. Instead, I stuffed my hands in my pockets and wished I was older and taller and had a girlfriend like Barbara to talk to.

The streetcar showed up in a couple of minutes. At this time of day, it was almost empty. Barbara and I sat near the front. While she looked out the window, thinking her own thoughts, I entertained myself reading ads: More doctors smoke Camels than any other brand. Pepsi Cola hits the spot, twelve full ounces that's a lot. Doublemint Gum—double the pleasure, double the fun.

Suddenly Barbara nudged me to get my attention. "See those?"

She pointed out the window at a row of houses going up on Rhode Island Avenue. "The one in the middle—right there—that's the one I want."

The house wasn't much more than a brick shell on a muddy lot, but Barbara showed me one on the corner that was nearly finished. "It will be like that," she said.

"It's nice," I said, but I hoped she wasn't expecting the house to solve everything. Unlike a true Smith, Barbara still believed she'd be happy someday.

22

THAT AFTERNOON, LIZARD AND MAGPIE SHOWED UP TO take Brent and June to the playground, which was a big relief. The troll had been driving me crazy all day. Read this, Yuncle Poopoo, read that, play horsey, build me a tower, and so on. Barbara never called him off once. She just sat there pounding the typewriter keys.

When I heard the Siamese twins coming up the stairs, giggling at every step, I hid in the bathroom. I had nothing to say to Lizard. She had nothing to say to me either, except her stupid wisecracks. I wasn't in the mood to be insulted. Not today.

When I was sure they'd all left, I peeked out the window. Lizard and Magpie were holding Brent's hands, and June was skipping along beside them, laughing at something Lizard was saying—probably a joke about me. It hurt to see my own sister getting a chuckle at my expense.

Barbara glanced up from her typing, but she didn't

say anything. Maybe I had one of those ugly looks on my face. I flung myself down at the other end of the table and opened my notebook. A couple of letters back, William had told me more about the new kid in Grandma's house. Her name was Linda, but he'd said not to get any ideas: "She's *not* my girlfriend, just a friend."

In my answer, I'd asked him what Linda looked like, especially in a sweater. "Have you ever kissed her? I know you said she wasn't your girlfriend, but that was a couple of weeks ago, maybe now she is."

In his next letter, William said he'd never kissed Linda, though he admitted he'd thought about it once or twice. "Most of the time, we talk," he wrote, "about books and movies and how we feel about things."

As for the way Linda looked in a sweater, he hadn't really noticed. "The same as any other girl, I guess" is how he put it.

The first thing I told him in my letter was,

You need new glasses, William. Believe me, all girls don't look the same in sweaters, some are bigger than others if you know what I mean. If you think about kissing Linda, you should go ahead and do it. She just might like it.

I looked at what I'd written. Who was I to tell William about kissing? The one girl I'd kissed had slugged me so hard she'd made my nose bleed. Maybe he should stick to talking. It was probably a whole lot safer.

So I added, "Maybe you should ask her first and then, if she says yes, kiss her."

Next I told him about my weekend crime spree—stealing the record, getting thrown out of the dance, cherry bombing the professor's house, getting suspended. But when I read it over, it sounded like a big joke. Something to laugh about with Toad and Doug, something to brag about.

"The truth is, I wish I had somebody like Linda to talk to," I wrote.

But Stu's always studying, Barbara's got her hands full, June's too little, and Toad and Doug are just plain dumb. If Lizard was like Linda, I'd tell her stuff I don't tell anybody. Like how mad I am all the time, how everything makes me sore, how—

While I sat there trying to decide what to say next, I heard June and Brent thundering up the steps. I got ready to hide in the bathroom, but Lizard didn't come with them.

June peered over my shoulder. "Is that a love letter to Elizabeth?"

I covered what I'd written and gave her a dirty look. "Of course not. Do you think I'd waste my time writing to that snob? She hates my guts."

"She asked where you were when we were at the playground," June said. Then she covered her mouth with her hand. "Oops, she told me not to tell you."

I stared at my sister. "What else did she tell you not to tell me?"

June giggled and picked up my pencil. Without

looking at me, she started drawing a picture of a horse. "She and Margaret were talking about the trouble you got into at the dance. Elizabeth said Bobby was a jerk, and Margaret said, 'What about Gordy, is he a jerk, too?' Then they both started giggling."

I stared at June, suddenly interested. "Did Lizard say anything else about me?"

June frowned and erased the horse's legs. "They don't look right, do they? I wish horses didn't have such fancy legs. They're so hard to draw."

I took the pencil. "What did Lizard say, June?"

She reached for the pencil. "Nothing. She saw me standing there and told me not to tell you what I'd heard—or else." June ran a finger across her throat like she was cutting it with a knife.

I sighed and handed her the pencil. "The next time Lizard talks about me, don't get caught listening. Come home and tell me every word. Okay?"

"Gordy and Elizabeth sitting in a tree," June chanted, "K-I-S-S-I-N-G." That made her howl with laughter.

When she recovered, she went back to work on the horse. She was right—the legs were all wrong. And so was the neck, but I didn't tell her. No sense hurting her feelings.

After she'd worn a hole in the paper with her eraser, June threw the pencil down and went out to the kitchen to pester Barbara for a cookie.

I sat at the table for a while, thinking about Lizard calling Pritchett a jerk. Though it didn't seem possible, I couldn't help wondering if she'd sent the note to

Mueller. But why would she do that? She hated me.

A few minutes later, Stu came home. Without even giving the poor guy a chance to take off his jacket, Barbara launched into a full report of what had happened in Mueller's office. Though Stu was upset at me for being suspended, he was surprised to hear Pritchett had gotten the same punishment. Like me, he'd expected Pritchett to get away with a reprimand at the worst.

"I have news, too," Stu said finally, looking straight at me. "I went to the horticulture department this afternoon and talked to Professor Whitman."

I chewed my thumbnail, too scared to ask if I was going to reform school.

Barbara asked for me. "Is he pressing charges?"

Stu looked at me. "He's decided to put you to work instead, Gordy. Starting Saturday, you'll be doing chores for him. He needs some help building a rock garden. After that, he—"

While Stu talked about turning compost piles, digging a garden, and other fun projects, I let my breath out in a long sigh of relief. Anything was better than reform school, I told myself. Even hard labor in Whitman's yard.

23

I SPENT MY TWO DAYS OF SUSPENSION ENTERTAINING THE troll while Barbara caught up on her typing. The morning I was supposed to go back to school, the kid had a fit.

"But Dordy, who will read me 'tories and play horsey?" he asked.

It was the first time he'd used my real name. Could it be that Brent was finally warming up to his old yuncle? I grinned and gave him a pretend punch on his arm, just like Donny used to do to me.

"Don't worry, Brent," I said. "Sooner or later I'll be under house arrest again."

Barbara glanced at me and I winked, hoping she'd know I was just saying it to get the troll off my back.

I left the apartment, glad to be free, and met Toad and Doug at the streetcar stop. I talked to them, even sat with them on the streetcar, joking, laughing, and cutting up like everything was back to normal. But nothing seemed natural. I was playing the part of this dope named Gordy, mouthing off about all the fun I'd had being suspended, bragging about what I'd do to Pritchett and Whitman when I had a chance, and so on, but what I said and did with Toad and Doug just didn't matter anymore. They'd let me down for the last time. I'd never trust either of them again.

Lizard was sitting a few seats ahead of us. Whenever I laughed or talked loud, she'd glance over her shoulder at me. Then she'd whisper to Magpie. The more she looked, the louder I laughed.

By the time Pritchett and his friends joined the fun, Toad, Doug, and I were making so much noise, the driver was threatening to throw us off. That quieted us down some, but I noticed Pritchett took a seat in the front, well away from both me and Lizard. He didn't look at either one of us. Just sat there talking to his friends and ignoring me and everyone else, the snob.

When I got off the streetcar, Pritchett was halfway to Route 1, and walking fast. "See that?" I said to Doug and Toad. "The coward's scared to meet up with me. Without Jackson to protect him, he—"

"Oh, grow up, G.A.S." Lizard gave me a look and swept past with Magpie.

I watched her march up the street ahead of me. She didn't look back once, no matter how loud I laughed. Girls—there was no pleasing them.

Usually I only saw Lizard at lunch, but that day I ran into her at least three times in the hall. She glanced at me but she didn't speak—just kept going, swinging that hair of hers. In the cafeteria, every time I looked at her, she was looking at me. Even Doug noticed.

Finally I walked right up to her and said, "Why do you keep looking at me?"

She blushed. "I don't."

"Yes, you do. You were staring at me just a couple of seconds ago. I saw you."

"Maybe it's because you're so ugly. Like a dead skunk in the road—you don't want to see it, but something makes you look anyway."

Magpie started snickering, which encouraged Lizard to add, "You look at me too, G.A.S. If you didn't, you wouldn't see me looking at you!"

"I wouldn't ruin my eyesight on you." With that, I walked out of the cafeteria. Behind me, the Siamese twins went on giggling.

That afternoon, I reported to Mueller's office. Pritchett was already there. We exchanged looks but didn't say anything—not with Mueller sitting a few feet away, watching us. We opened our notebooks and did our homework. The only sound was our pencils scratching across the paper.

When we left school, Mueller walked outside with us, making remarks about the weather—warm for March, probably would rain tomorrow, stuff like that. He didn't fool me. He was there to make sure the two of us didn't get into another fight.

No chance of that—Old Lady Pritchett was waiting in her fancy Buick. I noticed she didn't smile or wave at Mueller. No more bridge games, I guessed, no more country club stuff.

I walked to the streetcar stop and rode back to College Hill all by myself. Read the ads again, stared out the window, and thought about Lizard. Why did she look at me so much? Did it mean she liked me a little bit? Or did she still hate me? How could I tell?

Saturday morning I trudged to the professor's house and rang the doorbell. I'd hoped it would be pouring down rain so I wouldn't have to work on the rock garden, but it was the kind of warm, sunny day that made people shake their heads and say, "When March comes in like a lamb, it goes out like a lion." Meaning if the month starts out good, it will end rotten—like most things.

Mrs. Whitman opened the door and smiled. "Come in, Gordy. Roland will be down in a minute."

I followed her into the living room and took a seat on the edge of the couch. The room reminded me of Mrs. Sullivan's house. China shepherds and shepherdesses perched on spindly tables, the kind that tipped over if you brushed against them. Larger figurines kept watch from the mantel. Doilies covered chair arms and backs. The air smelled of furniture polish and window cleaner. I was afraid to move for fear of breaking something.

Then the professor appeared in the doorway. He was wearing a white T-shirt and a pair of old khakis. His belly hung over his belt. He had on loafers but no socks, and he hadn't gotten around to shaving yet. He looked even more out of place in the living room than I did.

"Well, Smith," he growled, "you're not as big as I remembered. Let's hope you're stronger than you look."

I forced myself to keep my mouth shut—which was a good thing, because what I wanted to say was so bad it might have made Whitman mad enough to send me to reform school after all.

"Don't give me the evil eye, boy," Whitman said. "When I finish with you, you'll have bulging biceps in those skinny arms. Why, you'll look like Gorgeous George himself."

Without giving me a chance to answer, he led me outside and pointed to a pile of boulders in the backyard. Every one of them must have weighed more than I did. "I had these dumped here last year for a rock garden," he said, "but I haven't gotten around to moving them yet. Bad back, you know. Old war injury."

Whitman pressed his hands to the small of his back and gave me a hard look. "Most Americans were proud to serve their country."

I kept my face as stony as his. "My brother Donny was in the Battle of the Bulge."

"I was in Sicily," Whitman said. "That's where I was wounded. Got a Purple Heart."

I nodded, but I didn't say anything. Every soldier who took a bullet got a Purple Heart. Nothing special about that. Too bad Donny hadn't won the Medal of Honor. That would have shut Whitman's mouth.

The professor went on talking about the war, describing this campaign and that campaign, while I stood there waiting to hear what I was supposed to do with the rocks. It was amazing how boring he made the battles sound.

Finally he handed me a shovel and led me around to the front yard. "Dig up this area first." He pointed at stakes he'd pounded into the ground, marking out an area about six feet square. "Dig down about two feet. Turn over the soil. Get it nice and loose. Then I'll show you where to put the rocks."

I hadn't expected an easy job, but it was even worse than I'd imagined. My own back would be ruined by the time I dug up the ground and hauled the rocks around front. And I wouldn't even have a Purple Heart to show for it.

The professor grinned and slapped my shoulder. "The beauty of it is, there won't be a kid—including you, Smith—who can sled across my yard next winter without hitting the rocks."

With that, Whitman walked off to the house, leaving me to do the dirty work. I had to hand it to him. He'd come up with a punishment that fit the crime.

24

As the weeks passed, I got used to Whitman. For an old guy, he had a pretty good sense of humor. Sometimes he actually made me laugh. He knew how to tell a good joke, but not the kind I could pass on to a girl.

There was no denying he drank like a fish. I hardly ever saw him without a bottle in his hand. The garbage can was full of dead soldiers, as Donny used to call the old man's empties. You'd think Whitman was still killing off the Nazis.

Mrs. Whitman didn't approve of the professor's ways. She was always giving him peeved looks and making comments like, "That's your third beer, Roland, and it's not even one o'clock yet."

He never paid any attention to her, except to pat her rear end and say, "Oh, Hazel, relax. A few beers never hurt anybody."

That's what he thought.

One afternoon, I was wrestling boulders into place

in the rock garden. Whitman was watching me from the front steps, a bottle of beer in his hand as usual. It was a warm day, and I was sweating up a storm, but I felt good. Almost happy. The week before, the money had come from Grandma's estate, and Stu had made a down payment on the house Barbara wanted so bad. Hard to believe, but soon I'd have my own room in the basement, just like Barbara had said. Privacy at last.

While I was struggling to lift an especially heavy rock, I saw Lizard walking along the streetcar tracks that ran past the Whitmans' yard. At school, she still looked at me from time to time, but I hadn't had a chance to talk to her for ages. She and Magpie had joined the chorus for the spring musical, and they were always at practice. They didn't even have time to take Brent to the playground.

But there she was, all by herself, looking in every direction but Whitman's yard. It was a warm sunny day, and she was wearing a white blouse and a pair of blue shorts. Grandma would have said she was rushing the season, but with legs like hers Lizard could rush all she wanted.

Without thinking, I whistled long and low—I just couldn't stop myself.

If Lizard hadn't seen me before, she sure saw me now. Glaring down at me from the tracks, she said, "Get fresh with me, G.A.S., and you'll be sorry."

"Can't blame the boy for admiring a pair of good-looking gams," Whitman said between swigs. "If I were Gordy's age, I'd whistle, too."

Lizard's face turned scarlet and she started to walk away, snippy little nose in the air, rear end swinging.

I stood there with the shovel in my hand, staring after her. As usual, I'd cooked my goose. And the professor had helped me do it.

Whitman winked at me. "You've done enough hard labor for today, Smith. Those rocks aren't going anywhere. But that cute little gal is. I'd go after her if I were you."

He didn't need to tell me twice. Dropping the shovel, I ran after Lizard. "Hey," I called, "wait up, will you?"

"Why should I?" she yelled without looking back or slowing down.

I managed to get in front of her and block the path. "Don't be mad, Lizard. Whitman's crocked as usual, he didn't mean anything."

She looked me in the eye. "What's *your* excuse?"

"Me? I was just whistling while I worked—you know, like the three little pigs."

"It's the seven dwarfs who whistled," Lizard said. "Not the three little pigs."

"Huh?"

"In *Snow White*, dummy. The dwarves whistled while they worked."

"Come on, Lizard, don't be sore."

She gave me a mean look. "Get out of my way, G.A.S."

I stepped aside, but I didn't leave. "Where are you headed?"

"No place special."

"Me either." I strolled along beside her. It was a free country. I had just as much right to walk along the streetcar tracks as she did.

I expected her to tell me to get lost or something, but she didn't say a word—just kept walking like it was normal for us to be together.

"See that house right there?" I pointed to the Smith family's future home. It was nearly finished now, at least on the outside. "We're moving in May."

"Barbara told me that a long time ago," Lizard said.

I shoved my hands in my pockets and tried to think of something else to say. Nothing came to mind. It wasn't easy talking to girls.

"So how do you like working for Professor Whitman?" Lizard asked after a while. "Is he as crazy as everybody says?"

I shrugged. "He's not so bad. Drinks a lot, though."

Lizard stepped on one of the rails and walked along, balancing herself with her arms. I hopped onto the other rail and staggered along beside her.

"Daddy told me you could've gotten in big trouble throwing those cherry bombs," she said. "You were lucky Whitman let you off so easy."

"You try digging a bunch of rocks out of the ground and moving them someplace else, along with a ton of dirt. Then tell me I got off easy."

"Oh, poor G.A.S.," Lizard said. "It's better than reform school, isn't it?"

I glanced at her. "Your father was pretty decent about the whole thing," I said. "Knowing what you think of me, I thought he'd lock me up and throw away the key. Get rid of G.A.S. forever."

Lizard didn't look at me, didn't say anything either. She just wobbled along like she was crossing the Grand Canyon on a tightrope. If she took her eyes off the track, she'd fall to her death.

By now we'd reached Garfield Road. Lizard's house was a couple of blocks to the right, and the playground was a couple of blocks to the left. I figured she'd say good-bye and go home, but she stood on the track, arms outspread, chewing gum so hard I could see her jawbone move under her skin.

"Want to go to the playground?" I asked her.

"What for?"

I shrugged. "Something to do."

She thought a minute. "Okay."

We walked up Garfield Road together, Lizard and me. I noticed the buds on the maples had turned red and the willows' long branches were yellow-green with new leaves. A robin hopped around, pecking at the grass. Something smelled sweet—flowers, I guessed. Or maybe it was Lizard. Whatever it was, spring was definitely here—warm days, blue skies, sunshine.

A bunch of kids were playing on the ball field. One of them was Pritchett. When he got up to bat, Lizard and I both saw him hit an easy fly. Everybody on his team yelled at him. Three guys had been on base. What could have been a grand slam home run became the third out.

"Dope," Lizard muttered.

My heart gave a funny little hop and jump. "You really think Pritchett's a dope?"

"He had no right to say mean things about your family," Lizard said. "He shouldn't have hit you so hard, either. Your face looked the way it did in grade school when—"

She stopped and scuffed the ground with the toe of her sneaker. I guessed she'd said more than she'd planned to. "It made me mad," she muttered. "That's all."

I stared at her. "You wrote that note to Mueller, didn't you?"

"What if I did?" Lizard glared at me. "It was mainly because of Stu. What Bobby said wasn't fair. Stu's so nice, he's—"

"I can be just as nice as Stu," I cut in. "That is, if I want to be."

Lizard's blue eyes bored into me. "Hah. You couldn't be nice if you tried, Gordy Smith."

"I could so!"

Lizard chomped her gum and studied my face. "Prove it," she said. "Do something nice."

"Like what?"

She went on chewing, thinking hard. Finally she said, "You can start by calling me *Elizabeth*. That's my name, you know. Not Lizard."

"Elizabeth," I tried it once, then tried it again. "Eee-lizabeth. Uh-lizabeth." I shook my head. "It's too prissy—like a Puritan or something. And you're—well, you aren't—I mean, you . . ." I gave up. If I said the wrong thing now, she'd walk off and that would be the end of it.

Lizard thought a second. "Well, how about Liz? Does that sound better?"

"Liz." It wasn't nearly as hard to say as Elizabeth, but it still didn't fit her. "What about Lizzy? Do you like that?"

"Liz," she said. "Not Lizard, not Lizzy—*Liz*." She paused a second and added, "If you keep calling me Lizard, I'll call *you* G.A.S.—or, better yet, Yuncle Poopoo."

"Okay, *Liz*, okay. Anything you say, *Liz*. You're the boss, *Liz*." From the way she grinned, I guessed she thought she'd won. But the truth was, no matter what I called her to her face, she'd always be Lizard in my mind.

We walked to the sandbox and sat down next to each other on one of the wooden sides. Lizard scooped up a handful of sand and watched it run through her fingers.

"So where's good old Magpie today?" I asked. Not that I really cared. It was just something to say.

Lizard raised her head and frowned. "If you mean *Margaret*, say Margaret."

"Oh, come on, Liz."

"Call Margaret *Margaret*. She doesn't like Magpie any more than I like Lizard." She paused. "I mean it, *Yuncle Poopoo*."

I sighed. Girls—there was no satisfying them. "What if I call her Maggie?"

Lizard tipped her head to the side and thought about it. "Yeah," she said, smiling. "Maggie and Liz—that's what we'll call ourselves. It sounds more grown-up than Margaret and Elizabeth, don't you think?"

"I guess." I didn't really have an opinion on such things. Like I said, no matter what I called them out loud, they'd always be Lizard and Magpie to me. "So where is good old Maggie?"

"At the dentist." Lizard started drawing circles in the sand with a stick. Her hair swung forward and hid her face. I wanted to reach out and brush it back, but I had a feeling that might be a mistake.

Instead, I picked up a stick of my own and made a few doodles in the sand beside Lizard's. I wished I could say something to make her laugh, but sitting this close to her, I couldn't come up with a good wisecrack—or anything else. In desperation, I mumbled, "Nice day, huh?"

Lizard nodded, but she didn't look up from her little pile of sand. "It sure is."

That pretty much took care of the weather. It was a dumb subject anyway. What did William say he and Linda talked about? Books, movies, how they felt. I wasn't ready to spill my guts just yet, so I asked Lizard if she'd seen any good movies lately. That seemed safe.

"My brother, Joe, took Margaret—Maggie, I mean—and me to see *Song of the South,*" Lizard said. "It was soooo good. Especially the cartoon parts. I just love Disney movies."

After Lizard told me the whole plot of *Song of the*

South, I told her about *The Big Sleep,* my favorite movie. She wasn't crazy about Humphrey Bogart. Like most girls, she went for Cary Grant, Tyrone Power, and Clark Gable.

"Speaking of Clark Gable," Lizard said, faking a little swoon, "have you ever read *Gone With the Wind*?"

When I shook my head, she told me a little bit about the plot. The war part sounded pretty good, but the rest was definitely girl stuff. Hoping to improve her taste in books, I told her about *White Fang.*

And so it went. For the first time in our lives, Lizard and I were having a real conversation. She'd say something and I'd say something back. Like a tennis game—her turn, my turn. No insults. No dumb cracks. William was right—you could actually talk to girls, especially if you had one all to yourself.

When we ran out of books, I took a deep breath, looked Lizard in the eye, and said, "Would you like to go to the movies with me sometime?"

I tried to sound like it didn't matter whether she said yes or no, but my voice came out as squeaky as one of June's doll babies.

"*The Yearling*'s coming to the Hyattsdale Movie Theater next month," Lizard said. "I saw the previews last Saturday. It looked pretty good."

"Does that mean you'll go with me?"

Lizard smiled one of those heart-stopping smiles she was so good at and shrugged. "Maybe."

She hadn't said yes, she hadn't said no, but something in her eyes told me we'd soon be sitting in the dark side by side, eating popcorn and watching a movie. A sad one, too, from what I'd heard—so sad Lizard might need comforting.

The biggest grin I'd ever grinned spread across my face. I wanted to jump up and run laps around the baseball diamond, climb the tree beside the sandbox and shout "Hooray" from the very top, make a long-distance call to William and say, "Hey, I've got a girlfriend, too."

Of course, I didn't do any of those things. I sat where I was, trying to act like nothing special had happened. After all, I hadn't forgotten I was a Smith—which meant I had to be on the lookout for bad things around the corner. It didn't pay to be too happy.

I glanced at Lizard. She was drawing in the sand again and humming the "Too-Fat Polka." I wanted to kiss her, but I was too scared of messing things up to try. So I took a deep breath instead and let it out slow and easy.

No matter what happened to me in my life, I knew I'd never forget this day and how it felt to sit and talk with Lizzy the Lizard. Liz, that is—Liz Crawford.

MARY DOWNING HAHN is the award-winning author of many popular books for young readers, including two previous books about Gordy: *Stepping on the Cracks*, winner of the Scott O'Dell Award for Historical Fiction, and *Following My Own Footsteps*. A former librarian, an avid reader and traveler, and an all-around arts lover, Ms. Hahn lives in Columbia, Maryland.

www.MaryDowningHahnBooks.com

MARY DOWNING HAHN is the award-winning author of many popular books for young readers, including two previous books about Gordy: *Stepping on the Cracks*, winner of the Scott O'Dell Award for Historical Fiction, and *Following My Own Footsteps*. A former librarian, an avid reader and traveler, and an all-around arts lover, Ms. Hahn lives in Columbia, Maryland.

www.MaryDowningHahnBooks.com